TimeLocke

BY THE SAME AUTHOR

LockeStep

HammerLocke

TimeLocke

A JOHN LOCKE MYSTERY

Jack Barnao

Charles Scribner's Sons
New York

Maxwell Macmillan Canada, Inc.
Toronto

Maxwell Macmillan International
New York   Oxford   Singapore   Sydney

Charles Scribner's Sons
Macmillan Publishing Company
866 Third Avenue
New York, NY 10022

Maxwell Macmillan Canada, Inc.
1200 Eglinton Avenue East,
Suite 200
Don Mills, Ontario M3C 3N1

Macmillan Publishing Company is part of the
Maxwell Communication Group of Companies.

This is a work of fiction. Names, characters, places, and incidents either are the product of the author's imagination or are used fictitiously. Any resemblance to events or persons, living or dead, is entirely coincidental.

Library of Congress Cataloging-in-Publication Data
Barnao, Jack.
    TimeLocke : a John Locke mystery / Jack Barnao.
        p.   cm.
    ISBN 0-684-19298-5
    I. Title.
PR9199.3.B3717T5   1991
813'.54—dc20   91-11582

10 9 8 7 6 5 4 3 2 1

Printed in the United States of America

For Salvie, the veteran Barnao,
with affection and respect

TIMELOCKE

CHAPTER

1

I EARNED my keep in the last hour of a seven-day assignment. That was typical. The opposition knew that Melanie Keene had a bodyguard, so they didn't try anything right away. They let me go through the motions, escorting her to her car, standing around her trailer while she had her face done over for the next scene, lounging just out of camera range when she was working. Enough routine boredom that most guys start to coast, start doing things by the feel instead of by the book. Why not, anyway? I only had Melanie's word for it that she'd been threatened by an extortionist. It could have been a publicity caper.

Then, on the last evening of her time in Toronto, she decided she should mingle with her fans. I did my best to talk her out of it, and by then we were close enough that she was listening to me a lot of the time. But I guess she needed her fix of adulation. Or maybe she'd built up enough confidence in John Locke Personal Assurance. Either way, she overruled me.

So, with a quarter of an hour to fill before she hopped the limo for the airport, she went downstairs to the bar of the Edinburgh Towers, where the stargazers hang out waiting for things like this to lighten their lives. And they were there in force.

The piano player dropped the Barry Manilow dirge he was tinkering with and launched into the theme of her Academy Award—nominated movie of two years previously. The stand-up crowd took their cue, and she swept in to applause. The whole thing was about as spontaneous as the four-minute ovation Gorbachev gets from the Presidium, but she ate it up.

I was a half step behind her. Maybe a few people figured I was her date. I'm thirty-two, fifteen years younger than her, although you'd be hard put to know it when she's wearing full warpaint, as she was that night. And I had my Brooks Brothers suit on, the one I'd picked up on the last job to take me to New York, so I looked presentable. Anyway, I used the idea as cover, beaming and acting modest as I checked the crowd. Somebody here was likely to take a slash at her face with an open razor, or worse. That's what the threat had been: Your face is your future; think about that when you look in a mirror.

The crowd was yuppy, mostly gay. With three marriages and a couple of stints chez Betty Ford behind her, Melanie had the same kind of claque that Judy Garland used to have, especially among homosexuals. A whole crowd of them had turned out to sip expensive water and wait around on the chance of getting to breathe her air. They pressed forward, calling out greetings and extravagant compliments. But there were a couple of guys who weren't clapping. Those were the ones I watched while a waiter appeared and handed us our drinks, champagne for her, Canada Dry club soda for me. I had promised myself a double Bushmills Irish whiskey later, when she was on her plane and out of my charge.

The fans crowded around, most of them with menus or papers for her to autograph, and she was signing and smiling. Then one of the men I'd noticed came closer. He was back about three people from her, carrying a paper in his left hand, but he still had his glass in his right.

I slid between the worshipers and came up to him as if I were heading on to the men's room. He ignored me, and I tipped an ounce of my soda water into his glass.

It boiled up like lava, spitting acid all over his hands and up into his face. He yelled and dropped the glass, spilling its contents down his leg. This made him hop and scream, hurting too badly to run away. But I wanted him immobilized, so I gave him a discreet smash in the kidneys. He fell, and I went for the other guy. He was making for Melanie, but I kicked him behind the knee, and he buckled. I shoved him down and knee-dropped on his spine and frisked him, finding a straight razor in his top pocket. He was facedown on the carpet, struggling, but I chopped him across the back of the neck with my right hand, and he went limp.

I was on my feet instantly, watching for more trouble. But it was over. The hotel security man was in the room, and he had grabbed the first creep, the one with the acid on him. The guy was screaming like a burning horse, and the rest of the crowd was yelling and hissing with fear and astonishment. One of them was keening and holding his hand over a burn on his wrist. He was going to sue, I learned as I relieved the house dick, who ran for the phone.

One of the bar patrons stooped down past me. "I'm a doctor," he said. I glanced up. My charge was safe. One of her fans had gotten the message and had taken his jacket off, ready to cover her if anyone tried a reprise. I took a moment to tell the doctor, "It's acid; he was after Miss Keene."

"Then he deserves what he got," the doctor said grimly, but he was using his beer to wash the acid off the man's face as he spoke.

"Hold him," I said, and grabbed the water jug off the bar. Angel of mercy Locke. I wondered what this guy thought of his occupation right now. It didn't have the same appeal it had held when he came in here, I figured.

The house dick was back within seconds, and I headed for Melanie. Her fan was disconcerted. He was a good-looking guy. Maybe he was hoping to be discovered. I gave him a big smile and spoke to her. "Let's go, Miss Keene. They can clean this up without you." To the guy I said, "Thank you, sir, you were very quick. Tell the detective what you did."

That bought him off, along with the smile Melanie flashed him. He turned away, and she looked up at me, holding her left hand on her heart, cupping her breast as if she didn't know the effect it had on every male hormone in the room. "The bastards. They were trying to scar my face," she whispered, and I thought, *Prince of Darkness*, the nightclub scene.

"Let's go before the police get here," I said, keeping a big smile on my face. She stood up, and I steered her to the door with my left hand, making sure I had a clear sweep at my gun with the right. There was a chance yet that this team comprised all Three Stooges. It didn't seem likely. Two big strong men should have been plenty to damage one small woman, especially when one of them had a jug of hydrochloric acid.

I whisked her into the elevator and pushed her into a

corner, behind me, until the doors closed. Then I eased up a fraction. "Are you all right?"

"Yes." She wasn't acting now. She was trembly but tough. "Thanks to you. How did you know?"

"You can tell," I said.

"But what did you do? Nudge him, what? How come he burned himself?"

"I was just testing. If he'd been holding a drink, nothing would have come of it. But if you add water to acid, it boils. It boiled up over him."

"Thank you, John," she said soberly. "You saved me."

"Just gave new meaning to the expression 'saving face,' " I said cheerfully. "Now stand behind me when the door opens."

She did as she was told, and I got off first and checked the corridor. There was nobody waiting, and I handed her the key. "Let yourself in. I'll keep my hands free."

She did it while I watched the corridor, and when we were inside, I slipped the chain on and said, "Sit down. Would you like a drink of water?"

"Please," she said, and sat down. Her dresser came out of the bedroom, surprised, and Melanie smiled weakly at her. "A change of plans, Juanita. I'm going to wait here for the limousine."

I left them talking details while I got her the glass of water and then checked with the front desk. A couple of cops had arrived to take the two guys into custody. The detectives would be coming up soon, I was told, but Melanie shook her head at that one. She couldn't wait while an investigation plodded to its end. She had a meeting with a producer in L.A. the next morning, and she was going to be on her plane no matter what. I didn't argue. It probably meant one of the guys would get a free trip to Hollywood to take her statement. Most cops I've known would be delighted at that prospect. I asked the desk to hold the limousine until the house detective was free and have him stand by it until we came down. As I hung up, I noticed an acid burn on the cuff of my jacket.

"Hey. He spoiled my threads," I said, half-kidding.

"I'll replace it," Melanie said crisply. "And there's a two-grand bonus in this for you. Tell Sol I've okayed it." She was all business. We had spent the last three nights together, but she gave no sign. The attack had forced her outside herself. She was a survivor, checking the state of the crew of the lifeboat. I admire that kind of sense.

The detectives arrived within minutes, and one of them rode to the airport with us, taking Melanie's statement. Mine he would get later, he told me. She expanded for him, acting tough but scared. I could imagine him in the squad room later, telling everybody what a ballsy broad she was.

News of the attack had got out, and by the time we reached the airport, there were reporters and TV cameras as well as an extra contingent of fans. It didn't figure that anyone would try anything in front of all that media coverage, but I stayed alert while Melanie blew kisses and told everyone what a wonderful bodyguard I was. Good publicity except that my head was bobbing around the whole time, checking for danger. I must have looked a little spastic. Anyway, she paid me off with a kiss before she left the limelight, and I escorted her through to the aircraft and saw her aboard. I was carrying my Walther PPG, but the airport security chief is a friend from my army days, and he's given me a pass that skates me around the difficult bits. So twenty minutes later I was out in the concourse, unnoticed except for the detective. I was unemployed again, but I had five grand in receivables plus the price of a new suit. And who could tell? Perhaps a wealthy client would see my face on the eleven o'clock news. I took the detective to the bar and ordered us both a double Bushmills while he took my statement. Not the worst of days, I decided.

CHAPTER

2

I WAS HOME in time to watch myself on the eleven o'clock news. I didn't think other viewers would have noticed me, not with Melanie Keene sparkling like the Fourth of July. But the newspeople used the portion of film where she mentioned my name and said what I'd done for her, and later the anchorwoman used the reference to fill in one of those flat spots that happen sometimes when there's still some time left over at the end of the news. "A pretty nifty guy to have around, that John Locke," she said, and her partner, a guy whose hairdresser deserves an Emmy, said, "You got that right, Pam," and they both chuckled. There! Fame! Another fourteen minutes and Andy Warhol will be right about me.

When the news ended, I switched off the TV and sat, trying to come down from the combat high I'd worked up. It was hard, even with the faint strains of Mozart's Horn Concerto in E Flat filtering up through the floor from Janet Frobisher's apartment downstairs. If ever she switches to acid rock, I will have to move out, but her choices sit well with me, even close to midnight, and I slowly found myself decompressing. After a while, I gave up on my book and put the lights out so that I could sit looking out over the treetops in the backyard toward the lighted towers of downtown Toronto, thinking about the guy in the hospital with acid burns.

I wasn't sorry for him. He'd hired on without qualms to destroy Melanie's face and career, but I wondered whether his boss was going to take the setback personally and come after me. That was the flip side to the free publicity. Anybody with a grudge would know whom to look for.

The phone startled me. I put the light back on and answered with a nice neutral "Hello."

"Well done, John." It was my mother, sounding, as she always does, like a more dignified version of Queen Elizabeth.

"Thank you. You saw the news? I thought this was past your bedtime."

She let that go by, and I waited for the attack to start. Praise from her is rare. She has never forgiven me for getting kicked out of university, two of them in fact. Harvard and Cambridge, places I'd never have gotten close to except for the family money. And, on top of that, ignoring the family company and joining the British army for the excitement. Well! I can still remember the way her lips pursed at the thought.

"No, not tonight. I wanted to see the news about the building fund. Did you catch that, or were you too swept away with your own appearance?"

"I see you've reached the three-quarter mark. Congratulations." She deserved it. She was doing her best to rebuild Sick Kids' Hospital with her own hands, both of them sunk to the elbows in the pockets of anyone she could get to listen.

"Yes. We're making progress. Anyway, I was at the

home of another committee member, and then we saw the announcement about you and that horrid little man with the acid. I was"—she paused, searching for a smaller word than *proud*—"quite pleased. One of the women made some comment about your appearance, and I volunteered the fact that you're my son. She was almost—" Another pause.

"Impressed would do, Mother. I earned my keep tonight."

"I suppose so." This was vintage Mother. I didn't have a degree. The only letters after my name are M.C. for the Military Cross I won with the SAS in the Falklands war. I'm male enough to be proud of that, but my mother has never acknowledged my military service. Soldiers are bums. My medal makes me a decorated bum.

"Well, thank you for calling," I said, giving her the out I thought she was looking for. "I was thinking of coming over on Sunday. Is Dad still up among the polar bears?"

"Ellesmere Island, looking for oil. He won't be home for a month at least. Yes, Sunday would be nice. Why don't you come for tea? If you're not busy, of course."

"Should be fine. I don't have any assignments booked for the next few days," I minimized, and thought, Ever. My career, if you can call it that, was bumping along on the bones of its rear end, waiting for the phone to ring.

"Well, that's why I called, as a matter of fact. Mildred, that's my committee secretary, she has a daughter, bright little gal, as a matter of fact. She's a lawyer. Frightfully dedicated. Mildred despairs of her ever marrying."

"And you're nominating me for the job?" I guessed Mildred's daughter had thick legs—and glasses to match. My mother would never have offered to put me out to stud if she thought I might enjoy the work.

She didn't even sigh. I guess it was a sign of increasing respect. She was treating me the same way she treated my father, just pausing for a moment and then going on in the same tone of voice. She wears him down until his only possible answer is "Yes, dear." After which he heads north again on another of his geological expeditions. The Arctic can be a lot less chilly than my mother.

"You do make things difficult, John. We merely shared the thought that you two had a great deal in common and might find one another interesting."

"All we have in common is mothers who're into good works, Maw. Not the kind of background to build a life on."

"Really." Now she was miffed. "One just does what one can for the city one lives in. Anyway, I told Mildred I would give you her daughter's number. That hardly comes under the heading of solicitation."

"Fine, shoot." I picked up a pencil and wrote down the number. "Thanks for the vote of confidence. I'll give her a dingle in the morning."

"Good," she said. "Heaven knows it's time you grew up and settled down."

"I'm giving it my best shot," I said, but she had already grunted and hung up.

I put the phone down and moved off to the bathroom, feeling gloomy. I'm a bodyguard, not a gigolo. And lady lawyers are not the most enthusiastic partners I've come across. You pretty well have to read them their rights before you turn the lights out.

I cleaned my teeth and put out my own light just as the music ended below me. Nice timing, Janet, I thought. And then my phone rang again.

The man's voice was middle-aged, English, cultured.

"I'm sorry to disturb you at this hour. Do I have the Mr. John Locke who appeared on the television news this evening?"

"Yes, you do."

"Mr. Locke. My name is Wainwright. I was impressed by what I heard of your work and by the highly professional way in which you conducted yourself during the interview with Miss Keene." Miss, not Ms. or Melanie. I was right, this guy was a middle-aged Brit.

"That's kind of you, Mr. Wainwright." I kept my own voice cool. Professionals do not scuff their feet and say, "Aw shucks." Maybe this was a job.

His next question threw me. "Are you aware of the significance of the necktie you were wearing at the time?"

"Yes. I've earned the right to wear it." I'd been wearing my Brigade of Guards tie. My original entry to the British army was into the Grenadier Guards, although I spent most of my time with the SAS.

"Which regiment?" His voice had crisped at the edges. I could imagine him with a neatly trimmed mustache.

"Grenadiers, ten years, including some time seconded to another unit."

"Rank?" He almost barked it.

"First lieutenant." It's not high, but promotion is slow in peacetime, and you don't advance in your own regiment while you're spending years on duty with the SAS.

"Very good," he said almost gloatingly. "I have an assignment I would like to discuss with you. Are you free to travel?"

"For the right compensation, yes."

This produced an appreciative chuckle. "Very prudent. Why don't we discuss it in my office tomorrow? Would that be convenient?"

"It depends on the time," I lied breezily. Hell, I could always get my car washed another day.

"Eleven hundred hours," he said, and I did a small double take into the phone. What was he trying to prove? By the sound of his voice he'd been out of the army for thirty years at least.

"Eleven would be fine," I said. "Where's your office?"

He told me, and I repeated it and said I'd be there. And then I hit the feathers and slept like a baby.

I was up early for my run, putting in a brisk six miles while the streets filled with commuters headed in to start the day's nonsense with two hours of overtime. The sight cheered me. I wasn't one of them. I can't stand routine, and I've been in enough life-and-death situations that the pressures of business seem pathetically trivial. I hope to be able to avoid working steadily as long as I live. And with luck and an occasional assignment from the Melanie Keenes of the world, I'll do it.

I picked up the papers at the corner of Mount Pleasant and warmed down by walking the last block to my place, checking for coverage of the acid story. All three papers had it. The left-wing *Star* announced that the acid tosser had third-degree burns to his legs and speculated that he would sue me for assault. The business-minded *Globe and Mail* wondered whether the attack would have an adverse effect on the movie industry in Canada. But the dear old tabloid *Sun* had a picture of Melanie's kiss at the airport with the cutline "Hero's reward." That and a story that compared me with Sir Galahad and the guys at the hotel with Satan.

I showered while the coffee perked and then cooked myself a bacon-and-egg breakfast. Three mornings with a movie star in her room had left me OD'd on grapefruit.

After I'd completed the cryptic crossword in the *Globe,* I started getting ready, deciding what to wear to the meeting. I didn't want this guy to think I was some kind of military toy, never out of uniform. In the end I settled on a pair of buff pants and the leather jacket I'd picked up in Florence at a stall on the street behind the duomo. It usually lives in the trunk of my Volvo; it's scuffed up, but it's still the kind of jacket guys were getting swarmed for by our street gangs. It was probably more than I'd need for warmth. It was June 21, and we were getting the first of our summer weather.

I left the car behind. Wainwright's office was down in the high-rent district, where it costs more to park your car for an hour than it does to eat lunch. He was in one of the old buildings, no longer fashionable since the sixties, when our national banks started one-upping one another with the height of their head offices down here on King Street. The building Wainwright occupied was still bright and attractive, but it has a dated sadness to it, like a widow in a singles bar.

I went up to the nineteenth floor. It was five to eleven, but I wasn't going to skulk in the corridor like a jealous husband in a hotel, so I opened the door of 1931 and went in.

The receptionist was a machine-turned blonde of forty or so. She stood up when I came in. "You're Mr. Locke. I saw you on the news last night."

I gave a modest little snort and said, "I'm not usually so conspicuous. I'm here to see Mr. Wainwright, I'm a couple of minutes early."

She poured on the charm like maple syrup. "Mr. Wainwright said I was to show you in the moment you arrived. Come this way, please."

15

She made it sound like I'd get lost without her, but there was only one other door in the room. She went to it, inclining her head first to listen respectfully. Apparently she liked what she heard. She beamed at me, rapped on the door, then opened it and said, "Mr. Locke's here, Mr. Wainright."

She stood back, but before I could go through the door, Wainwright came out. The mountain was honoring Muhammad. He was tall and rangy, the way elderly men get when they work at staying youthful. I judged him to be about seventy. And I was right about the bristly World War II mustache. He stuck his hand out, smiling. "Mr. Locke. Thank you for coming in." His accent was more clearly English now but not regional. I know all the English tribal noises, and this wasn't one of them. His voice showed breeding and/or money. We shook, and he kept hold of my hand long enough to draw me into the room and close the door behind me. Then he let go and waved me to the chair across the desk from his. "Sit down, please."

I sat, glancing around the room. It didn't have the framed sheepskins that lawyers hang everywhere, and there were very few books on the shelves. He had a couple of photographs on his desk, but their backs were to me. On the walls he had a Lawren Harris landscape that looked as if it just might be the real thing and not a print. There was also a photograph of a French château.

"You like my office?" he asked dryly.

"I was thinking you'd make a good poker player, Mr. Wainwright. Nothing in here gives any hint of what you do. Unless you import wine from France."

He made an impressed face, the corners of his mouth turned down as he gave a brief nod. "Very good. What makes you think so?"

16

"You have that photograph of Chambord. It's on the Loire."

Now I had his full attention. "I see you know France," he said.

"One of my favorite countries, except for Paris, of course." To my mind, Parisians are the New Yorkers of Europe.

He chuckled. *"Parlez-vous français?"*

"Un petit peu," I said. "Enough to get *moutarde avec le jambon.*"

He chuckled again, humoring me, then said. "As a matter of fact, the assignment I had in mind for you is in Provence."

"I like it already. Whose body am I going to be guarding?"

He cleared his throat and hesitated for a moment. "I'm going to have some tea. Would you prefer Darjeeling or Lapsang souchong?"

"Whatever you're ordering, thank you. In ten years among the English, I never managed to develop a taste for the stuff."

He humphed and pressed the call button on his phone. The blonde appeared, smiling. "Jean, would it be possible to get some coffee, please?"

"Of course. I'll go downstairs," she said breathily, turning the full thousand watts on to me. "How do you like your coffee, Mr. Locke?"

"Black, please," I told her, and she vanished, looking as if she were about to burst with the excitement.

I sat and waited for Wainwright to break his news to me, wondering what the problem was. Most clients buy my services the way they buy steak. They know what they need. Their questions are about costs. I'm not used to people playing hard to get. He looked at me without speaking until it became a kind of showdown. Who was going to blink first? I broke the tie. "Can I infer, from your reluctance to speak, that this job you want me to do isn't legal?"

That cracked his coma. He shook his head. "No. It's perfectly legal, just unconventional." He picked up one of the photographs on his desk and handed it to me. It was a graduation photograph of a girl in her late teens, and she was beautiful, dark haired and intense looking, but with high cheekbones and a generous mouth that softened any hint of snootiness. She was smiling, and there was an air of mischief about her that for some reason made her seem Irish.

"She's lovely. And she also looks young to be getting a bachelor of arts from Cambridge."

"She was nineteen in that picture. That was six years ago. She's picked up her doctorate since. She's an historian."

"And she's working on the Roman history of Provence?"

He glanced up, impressed again. "You know about it?"

"History's kind of a hobby," I minimized. "I know they were there a long time. The Rhone was a highway for exports from Gaul, salt and wine mostly. I also know that the town of Vaison-la-Romaine has the biggest Roman ruins outside of Italy."

His voice was trancelike. "She's going to Vaison."

I handed him the photograph. "Well, unless somebody's got a contract out on her, she won't need my services," I said. "She'll be safer there than she would be in Toronto."

There was a tap on the door, and his secretary came back with the coffee. Wainwright made the most of the break, thanking her and praising her speed. I added an approving smile when she looked my way, and she left happily. Wainwright opened the coffees and then spoke as he handed me mine. "It's not a contract," he said. "It's more in the nature of a grudge."

"Perhaps you can spell it out for me." I sipped my coffee.

He left his untasted, seeming to be plucking up nerve. Finally, he said, "It started last year. She was over there, working in Vaison, and a film crew came to town." He shrugged helplessly. "I don't follow films at all, but they were working on some thriller or other, it seems, and they had a Corsican from Marseilles along with them as adviser."

"Some mob heavy?"

"Yes. The French tend to lionize their criminals, the way the Americans once did with Al Capone and his ilk."

I could see the story shaping up before he told it. Some jaded hood with a string of hookers available to give him the greatest sex money could buy and he'd flipped out for a clean-limbed beauty who was more concerned about dead Romans than she was about what shade of lipstick to use.

"And he put the moves on this young lady," I prompted when Wainwright bogged down.

"My niece," he said. "Her name is Amy Roger."

The name fit the photograph. Amy, a no-nonsense name. I'll bet that most girls her age are called Debbie. "He got fresh with Amy?"

"She was at dinner at the best restaurant in town with a friend, another historian. It's not a big place apparently, not grand." He waved his hand vaguely. "The film people were there, together with this man and his girl of the day. It seems he came over and tried to sit at Amy's table. He was drunk, and Amy brushed him off, politely but firmly.

It didn't work. He pulled a chair up beside her and made a grab at her. She slapped him, and when he tried to slap her in return, she hit him with the wine bottle."

I laughed. "Doesn't sound as if she needs a bodyguard, much as I'd like the job."

"It didn't end there," Wainwright said soberly. "One of the film people, a cameraman or something, he laughed at the man's discomfiture. That night he was hauled out of his hotel bed by two men, tied and gagged, driven into the countryside, where they broke both his arms."

"And what about Amy? What did she do?"

"She was staying with a very tough old Frenchwoman. She used to be with the Maquis, the Resistance. Amy told her what had happened, and she called out some old friends to guard the house with shotguns that night, and they drove Amy to the airport at Lyons the next day."

"How did she take that? I'd guess she was very annoyed at having her work interrupted."

"Indeed." Wainwright nodded and paused to take a sip of his coffee. "Fortunately, this all took place toward the end of her time there, so she didn't lose much in the way of fieldwork, but now she has to return for a few weeks on a new project."

"And the guy she hit is still mad," I finished for him.

"Yes." Wainwright set down his cup very carefully, as if he were afraid he would slam it down and splash it everywhere in sudden, uncontrollable anger. "I have a lot of contacts with the wine-growing establishment there, as everywhere in France, and the word is out that he intends to punish her, most severely."

"I can imagine what he has in mind," I said. "The Corsicans run most of the prostitution in southern Europe."

Wainwright couldn't let it rest there. "I'm afraid that if

she goes back there he will abduct her and abuse her and consign her to some North African brothel." His hands were shaking as he spoke.

"And you've tried to warn her but she's too committed to her subject to refuse to go on this trip."

He paused to mop his face with his handkerchief. "I can see I don't have to explain anything to you twice," he said.

I nodded, weighing the financial opportunity I had here. Damsels in distress are more fun to guard than rock stars or oil sheikhs, especially when they're as toothsome as Amy Roger. I would have taken the job for expenses alone, but my family did succeed in raising a businessman, even though they don't approve of my business. "Have you told her you'd thought of sending someone like me?"

He nodded grimly. "She was very angry. She said she would not allow this hoodlum to spoil her work. That was the first thing. And secondly, she did not want to have some muscle-bound oaf tagging along chewing gum and breathing beer on her."

"I hate being typecast," I said, and he smiled at last.

"You have no idea how relieved I was last evening to see you on the news," he said. "You're a man of culture; I think we can overcome her objections."

"At the risk of sounding mercenary, if we can persuade her that I'm housebroken, there is still the subject of compensation."

"I can't pay you as much as Miss Keene did," he said.

"Who told you what she paid?"

"I deal with some influential people in Canada as well as France," he said with a slight smirk. "From the owner of the Edinburgh Towers I got the name of Miss Keene's agent and hence, your fee structure."

"Your niece is a most interesting woman," I said softly,

"And the story you told me appeals to the knight-errant in my soul. But on the other hand, you don't have a whole lot of options open to you." There, I thought, ball in your court.

He held up his hand. "How does two thousand dollars a week for five weeks sound? Plus all expenses, of course."

"Fine." I nodded crisply, the way I'd learned to do when the officer in charge of the briefing told me what impossibilities he was expecting. No arguments. You do it. Period.

Wainwright extended his hand, smiling in relief, and we shook. Then he pressed the buzzer again. The sun shone from the doorway as the blond helmet came around the jamb. "Ah, Jean, would you be so kind as to make out a check to—" He paused and turned to me.

"John Locke, Personal Assurance," I said.

He nodded and turned back to her. "You have that?" She beamed, and he went on, "In the amount of five thousand dollars. Mark it on account of services to be rendered, fifty percent advance."

"Of course." She looked at me with a respect that showed me my attractiveness had entered a whole new dimension.

When she had gone, I said, "How do you propose to break the news to your niece?"

He sat, rocking slightly, his forehead pursed, an old man's gesture that made him look almost fragile. "I thought we might do it over dinner." He uncrinkled his brow and looked into my face. "What do you think?"

"Excellent. Would you like me to bring someone?"

"You have a wife?" He sounded surprised.

"No, but I do have a good friend who might be persuaded to make me look less threatening."

He nodded. "Good idea. Seven-thirty for eight, tomorrow evening at my apartment." He told me where it was located, and after his secretary had brought my check in for him to sign, we got the business out of the way, shook hands, and I left.

The day seemed a lot warmer with five grand in my pocket, and I ambled around the financial district, ducking into the underground shopping complex on King Street, where I spent a pleasurable half hour in the bookstore. After that, because I was in the district, I called the lady lawyer my mother had told me about. What the hell? I could buy her a bun down here on neutral turf.

Not surprisingly, she wasn't in, but I left a phone message and went on my way, feeling righteous. I had done my duty.

I banked my advance, keeping a modest couple of hundred out for walking-around money, then went to the central reference library and brushed up on the history of Vaison-la-Romaine before heading home. I got there just as Janet Frobisher drove up in her ancient Volkswagen beetle. She's tall and good to look at, with soft auburn hair. She's in her late twenties, and you'd figure she'd be a shoo-in to be out in the suburbs by now with a baby on each hip, but for some reason she's unlucky in her choice of men. I'm very fond of her and have been tempted a number of times, but the old superstition about doorsteps has always kept Janet and me on a brother-and-sister basis.

She works for our national radio network, the CBC, and when she saw me, she beamed and hoisted her purse aloft like a trophy. "Big day at the factory," she said. "I got the new digital tape of the Brandenburg Concerti. Would you like to hear it?"

"Love to." I said. "I'll head upstairs first and build us a couple of drinks."

"G and T, please," she said. "Give me ten minutes."

She lives on the second floor, and I live on the third, so I held the door for her and went up the back stairs behind her. Then I headed up to my own door, where I checked my security marker. It's not conspicuous, a hair just below the bottom hinge on the doorjamb. It's located at a distance of thirteen comb teeth from the bottom of the hinge, not a measurement anybody would be able to duplicate without the same pocket comb as mine. I hadn't been broken into. One of these days I will be. I've racked up enough black marks in the books of the PLO and the Provisional IRA that someone will get wind of me someday and I'll have to move, but for now, all was well.

After a quarter hour I ambled down to Janet's apartment with the gin bottle, tonics, and a couple of beers for me. She had changed out of her working skirt into blue jeans and racked up the tape. She let me in, then pressed the start button while I mixed her drink and opened a beer.

"The first concerto is my least favorite," she told me. "I was going to fix a spaghetti sauce while it's running, then listen to the rest. Would you like to eat with me?"

"Great," I said. "On one condition. Can I get you to come with me to a spiffy business dinner tomorrow?"

"Spiffy?" She raised both eyebrows. "Have you been dating cheerleaders again?"

"You know my principles. No girl with an IQ of lower than room temperature."

"Anything capable of reading and writing is in jeopardy," she said, laughing. "But what makes you think the occasion will be spiffy?"

"It's a prospective client. He imports French wine. I'd imagine he knows an escargot from a handsaw."

"Probably." She sliced onions, dashing at her eyes with her left wrist. "What's the occasion?"

"His niece is gun-shy. She's a historian, and she's tangled up with a bad-news Corsican. She's afraid I'll shoot somebody in the head and break her concentration when she's working."

"Tell me more," Janet commanded.

I sat there and gave her the whole rundown while she started the onions, then added the hamburger and garlic and her special choice of spices, finally tipping in a jar of the tomato paste she makes herself. Like I say, real wife-and-mother material. This night, she also had some feminine intuition for me.

"It sounds a little off if you ask me," she said, tasting the sauce.

"How so?" With five grand of Wainwright's money in my bank I didn't want discouragement.

"Well, let's say there's a few gaps in the story," she said. She put the spoon down and led me back to the living room to hear her tape. The second concerto is my favorite, but I interrupted it to hear what she had to say.

"Which areas of the story? Don't you think a guy like this Corsican might have made a pass at her?"

Janet shook her head impatiently. "Oh, no, I don't question any of that. What I'm looking at is the relationship between the man who approached you and this woman." She frowned. "Niece is a bit too easy. Does the girl have a father? And if she doesn't, why didn't he mention it?"

"He's a bit old to be the lover of a girl in her twenties. It would make damn near a half century difference in their ages."

"Thirty-five years isn't uncommon," Janet said. "I'm just saying that it doesn't ring twenty-four-karat true to my ear."

"Well, if you'll come with me tomorrow night, you can check him out for yourself," I said. "In the meantime, I've got his money, and you've got this wonderful recording of the Brandenburgs. Let's listen."

"Done," she said. "Can I trust you to wind it back to the beginning of the second while I check the stove?"

I turned the tape back, and we listened to music, then ate spaghetti and drank a bottle of red wine like an old married couple. At ten-thirty, we exchanged a chaste kiss at her door, and I said, "Thank you for a lovely evening. *Mañana*," and went upstairs feeling very domestic. That was when my phone went. I picked it up, and the lady lawyer said, "I know this is a hell of a time to call, but I've just finally uncovered the top of my desk and found your phone message. I was going for coffee and a doughnut. Does that sound like something you might enjoy?"

"Why not?" I said. Hell, I wasn't feeling that domestic.

CHAPTER

3

THE DOUGHNUT SHOP was a yuppie equivalent of the soda fountain where Archie and Veronica get together with Jughead and the kids. The only difference was that this one was filled with men and women in their twenties, dressed expensively, assembling here at the end of another sixteen-hour day before going on the town. Most of the bright-eyed geniuses in the place were sitting in front of a cup of black coffee, talking too loudly and wiping runny noses. I saw a guy at the counter who shook hands with most of them as they came in. Almost all his contacts went directly from him to the washroom and came out a minute later with a sniffle and a new lease on life. I also noticed that the guy left a twenty-dollar tip on the counter.

As far as I could tell, my own lady lawyer was clean. Her voice and deportment were normal, and she was taking cream with her coffee. She was sitting with a couple of live wires who suggested going on to some club or other, but the counselor took my advice instead, and she and I went on to a bar near the airport where Lou Rawls was performing.

In my car she said, "Thanks for coming down. Otherwise I'd have ended up in that same damn bar again, drinking Perrier and watching people I like getting high."

She smiled sadly as she said it. I wasn't convinced, but it's not my job to judge people. I just smiled back and said, "Glad we didn't go. I don't like hanging around folks on crutches." That had her seizing my arm as if it were a lifeline. Anyway, one thing led to another, and I was home by five with an updated reading on women in the legal profession.

After breakfast I got my car washed and went back to the reference library. They had promised to get me a transcript of Amy Roger's thesis. It had been reprinted in an English scholarly journal and become part of the literature of the Roman period in France. It was an account of the trade of her area of interest during the Roman occupation, esoteric stuff with none of the military details that make history an interest of mine. I ploughed through it, anyway. I wanted to look knowledgeable for the evening if she started riding her hobbyhorse.

In addition, I checked the Canadian *Who's Who* on Wainwright. There were no initial surprises. He had been born in England and been a regular army officer prewar, Irish Guards, having gone through Sandhurst, the British equivalent of West Point. But there were few details on his war service. He had served with a special unit of the British army and had received the Military Cross and the OBE. That's the Order of the British Empire, a decoration they give to spies. It meant he had been undercover somewhere, in France, I guessed. If he did business there, he was fluent in the language.

After the war he had started his wine importing company and had moved to Canada a few years later, presumably when his business blossomed here. He was a wheel on a number of cultural committees, the Toronto Symphony and Royal Ontario Museum board, and was active in char-

ity work, particularly for the United Way. It was all story-
book stuff except that there was no mention of any family.
It made me remember Janet Frobisher's doubts about him.

I was home before Janet and left a note on her door
reminding her of our dinner date. Then I went and changed
into gray slacks and a blazer. I wore a white shirt of Sea
Island cotton and the tie of my college at Cambridge. Amy
Roger would recognize it without my having to draw any
pictures for her. I hoped she wouldn't want to compare
academic careers with me. I didn't want to tell her I'd been
sent down, which is how you say expelled when you have
a stiff upper lip. My sin was unbecoming behavior with a
female history fellow. It was the story of my life prior to
the years I'd spent in the British army. I'd been a near
delinquent, and without the discipline and skills I'd learned
in uniform, I'd probably be another aimless waster right
now, shambling from one dreary job to another, drinking
my brains out, and hating my life. As it is, I'm happy inside
my skin. You can't buy that; you have to earn it.

On impulse I wore my gun. It's not conspicuous. I don't
affect a shoulder holster. They're useless, anyway. I wear
it at the left side of my belt, butt forward so I can do a
reach-around draw. The blazer is cut fairly full, so it doesn't
bulge. I figured that if we got to the "yes, but" stage of a
hiring discussion, I could let her see that I was tooled up
and she hadn't noticed.

At seven sharp I went down and knocked on Janet's
door. She opened it, looking handsome in a soft green dress
that set off the near red of her hair. Once again her appearance made me wonder why I didn't find somewhere
else to live so I could move in on her without feeling bad
about it.

"You look fantastic," I said. "Heavy date?"

She laughed. "Naah. I'm providing protective coloring for the playboy of the Western world."

"He's a fool if he doesn't propose," I said.

She touched me on the arm and said, "I know. Come on in. I promise not to tell him you said so."

We had a short drink. A glass of white wine for her, a Bushmills for me, and she asked, "Are you planning on taking something for our host?"

"At his income level it's not the done thing," I said. "It's déclassé to bring gifts; it suggests doubt that the host can afford the occasion."

"I've never moved in that rarefied atmosphere," Janet said. "I'm from a family of proles. We like to pay our way."

"Can't be done," I argued. "What can you take to the man who has everything? He imports wine; his cellar has to contain anything I could afford to take him."

She shook her head. "Men are so blind," she said. "I'll bet he's a music buff. How about a record?"

"I thought of that," I admitted. "But it comes in so many flavors these days—CDs, tapes, LPs. And besides, he may be tone-deaf."

"I despair of educating you," she said. "Grab some flowers. You can't just turn up empty-handed."

It was easier to agree than argue. "As long as you hand them to him," I said. "I've got to look capable of defending his niece. I can't carry a gun and a garland."

She laughed and called me a chauv, and we left, driving down past the Chinese grocery at Avenue Road and Davenport, where they have the best flowers in town. We arrived at his condo at twenty to eight. Security parked my Volvo while the doorman announced us and ushered us to the elevator.

We rode up eighteen floors, listening to wallpaper music that made Janet's eyes crinkle with amusement. "I think hell would be like this, only hotter," she said, and we both laughed.

Wainwright was waiting at the door of his apartment. He beamed as we came along the hall, looking at Janet with real warmth in his eyes. "Good evening. I'm Eric Wainwright," he said to her, ignoring me.

"Janet Frobisher. Delighted to meet you," she said, and Wainwright shook her hand, holding on to it for longer than was tactically necessary, his eyes sparkling with delight. He looked about ten years younger than he had in his office. Finally, he let go of her hand and shook mine, leading us into his lobby. It was high, anyway, and the ceiling was mirrored, so it looked endlessly lofty above us. He set down the flowers Janet had given him on the plinth of a reproduction of the *Winged Victory of Samothrace*, about four feet high but close to perfect. "John, how nice of you both to come," he said. "Come on in."

He ushered us down the hall to a long sitting room with big windows facing south over the Toronto Islands, a millionaire's view, very impressive. But more impressive was my first view of his niece. She was sitting on a couch opposite the windows, talking to a lean guy of around thirty, who was wearing a tweed jacket that bellowed "academic" loud enough to be heard down on the street.

He stood up when Janet came in, doing it with a practiced clumsiness so that the lucky girl is always going to think, He doesn't do this for everyone. I must be special.

Amy glanced at me first, then took a longer look at Janet. It seemed to me she was weighing the relationship between us, judging whether Janet had been brought in as a smoke screen.

Wainwright made the introductions. Amy, his niece, and her friend Peter Harrod. We all made the civilized noises, and then he poured drinks. Janet had white wine, like the other two, and then Wainwright turned to me and smiled. "You're a Bushmills man, right?"

"Right. Thank you," I said. God, was I that predictable? I carefully did not show any surprise. It would have looked vain and fluttery, as if my taste in booze were an exciting topic for all of us to discuss.

Wainwright didn't let it lie. "My spies are everywhere," he said happily. "You stayed at the Edinburgh Towers. That was all I needed to know."

I figured he'd earned an acknowledgment. "Were you in intelligence during the war, Major?" There, that would let him know I'd done my own homework.

He looked up alertly as he unscrewed a new bottle of Bushmills and poured me a double. "Not exactly," he said. "But you knew that, too, didn't you?"

Amy Roger laughed. "What is this, Eric, a game of one-upmanship? I thought we'd all been invited for dinner, not a battle of wits."

"You're going to get a fine dinner," Wainwright said. "You have to allow an old man his entertainments." He said it in a playful voice that was more than half-flirting.

We changed gears and chatted sociably about the difficulties of getting around town now that the tourist season was beginning. I was hoping this would lead to Amy's confessing that she was happy to be leaving town for the busiest part of the summer, but it didn't. She moved first, asking Janet what her plans for the summer were. I was impressed. She might be a bluestocking, but socially she was on top of her game.

Janet talked about her work in radio, and Amy Roger

gathered enough steam to move in on me. I detected an edge to her words. She had probably decided that Wainwright was bringing us all together for a purpose, and for her it was a reason to make a point of being unafraid and independent.

"Are you in broadcasting?" she asked.

"No, I'm kind of semiretired," I said.

Amy smiled. She had a very nice smile but didn't overdo it. "You seem a little young for retirement," she said. "I think you must have some profitable sideline."

"Kind of," I said. "I'm in the personal-assurance business, free-lance. I work as the fancy takes me."

This brought Amy's date to life. He had the standard academic's left-wing politics. "Insurance should be a government responsibility," he said.

"The line I'm in already is, for the most part," I said. "I take up the slack when police departments can't provide the protection my clients need."

"Police departments?" He frowned, wrinkling his face up like an apple doll. He looked like an impatient child. "Are police departments involved with insurance?"

"With personal assurance, yes," I said. "It's on all their vehicles. 'To serve and protect.' "

Amy explained for him. "Really, Peter. Mr. Locke is a bodyguard."

Harrod jerked his chin up almost angrily. "Good grief! Is there really a call for bodyguarding in this day and age?"

"Regrettably for some, fortunately for me, yes," I said.

Janet was watching the whole exchange straight-faced, but I could read her amusement. I've known her for a couple of years, and she's got a pretty good idea of my capabilities. On one occasion they'd been used to her advantage. Oddly, it was Wainwright who came forward with an explanation. I'd been expecting him to let me carry the ball on my own. "You may have seen John on the evening news a couple of nights ago," he said. "He saved his client from a very nasty personal attack."

"I never watch television," Harrod said automatically. "Was it reported anywhere?"

"Yes," Amy said, looking at me with a glitter in her eyes. "It was in the newspaper. Your client was Melanie Keene, the actress, wasn't it?"

"That's right."

Now Harrod frowned. "Oh, yes, that does ring a bell. You burned some poor chap with acid, didn't you?" His disgust was thick enough to cut.

"No. He burned himself with acid he was planning to use in disfiguring Miss Keene," I said. "It seems he was a leg breaker for a local loan shark." I deliberately kept the language rough-hewn to see Amy's reaction.

"Seemed unnecessarily violent, according to the report I read," Harrod said huffily.

"That's what I thought," I said kindly. "He would almost certainly have blinded her as well as destroying her face. But let's change the subject."

"Yes, let's do that," Harrod sniffed.

Amy was not so squeamish. "What did you do to him? Twist his arm?"

"I didn't touch him." I shook my head. "He dropped his glass, and it burned him, that was all."

Wainwright gave the subject another shove. "There were two of them, weren't there, John? Didn't the other one have a razor?"

"Yes," I said. "But Peter's right, Eric. No shoptalk in the mess, please."

That made Amy chuckle. "Are you another old soldier? You don't look old enough."

"I wasn't in at the same time as your uncle, but yes," I said.

"And was that before or after your stint at Sidney Sussex College?"

I made a surprised face. "Were you at Cambridge?"

"Yes. Trinity," she said. "What were you reading?"

"History. But I didn't take it very far," I said. "I understand that you did. You're a full-time historian."

"Yes." She said it with the same quiet pride you see in mothers when you compliment their children. "I like the view of life you get from a thousand-year or so perspective."

That gave Harrod his entry point, and he took over the conversation and brought us around to his own brilliance. I was relieved to find that his thing was the Thirty Years' War. It was more interesting to me than Roman France, and it also meant that he wasn't likely to be a stablemate of Amy's if she went to Provence.

Dinner was served by a self-effacing French woman who left as soon as the table was cleared, and we sat around with glasses of a very good cognac while Wainwright and Harrod smoked Romeo y Julietta cigars. "One of the few civilized things our disgusting government has done is maintain contact with Cuba," Harrod said through blue clouds of smoke. "A model socialist state."

I sipped cognac and said nothing. But Amy didn't let it rest. I had already formed the opinion that among the interests Harrod did not share with her was her bed. She was using him more casually than I would ever have used any woman I'd brought with me. "Do you agree?" she prodded me. "Surely you're not a socialist."

"I'm not much of anything," I said. "If you follow them far enough, left and right extremists can shake hands with one another at their furthest range. Both are funded from the same sources and train in the same places."

This made Harrod splutter indignantly, and we sat and listened to him until eleven, when Wainwright stood up abruptly and said, "Well, I'm going to bed now so that all you nice people can go home."

Amy and Janet both chuckled. I stood up. Harrod kept on talking until Amy tapped him on the shoulder. "That was last call, Peter. Be a dear and get my shawl."

"Do you have a car?" I asked.

"Good God, no," he said, laughing at the idiocy. "In this town? No. I go everywhere on my bicycle."

"And you're taking Amy on the crossbar?" I asked.

"We were going to take a taxi," he said.

"No need. We'll drop you off."

He protested, but Wainwright overruled him. "I'm sure John and Janet don't mind, old chap," he said. "I'll call security and they'll bring the car up for you."

That was when I was certain that he'd set something up. Perhaps he had even specified which partner Amy should bring home to dinner. He wanted us together in my car. He rang the front desk, but there was no answer. He hung up and turned back to us. "I'm sorry. The security man must be on his rounds. Would you mind getting your own car, John? All you have to do is press P1 on the elevator and go right down to the basement. Your key will be in the ignition, and the exit door opens automatically as you drive up to it."

"No problem," I said, and we all made our farewells. Wainwright stretched out his parting with Janet, asking if he might telephone her at work to get confirmation on the time of some broadcast she was preparing. She gave him her office number, and we all left.

Harrod was sulking but felt obliged to accept my offer, so he spent the elevator ride telling me how bad he felt about taking me out of my way. Amy chatted to Janet about the same broadcast, which she probably would not hear since it aired during the morning, when she was usually in the university library.

We got to the basement, and I stood back to let everyone out. It got into an Alphonse and Gaston routine with Harrod, but he left at last, and I followed them out, looking for my Volvo. It was parked at the end of a row. I pointed it out, and we headed toward it, the women walking in front. I was opening the doors for them when a man wearing a ski mask jumped out from behind another car. He was holding a black automatic.

"Gimme your wallets and purses," he said.

Janet and Amy both gasped in horror. Harrod said, "I say. What do you think you're doing?" and the man jabbed him in the chest with the gun. I wasn't scared. It was all too pat. Security at the door meant this shouldn't be happening. I figured Wainwright had arranged it. I stayed calm, breaking into my few words of Russian in a baffled tone. *"Prostite, pozhalista?"* I said, smiling stupidly. *"Kak ti delash?"* Excuse me, please, what are you doing? Not what Gorbachev's bodyguard would have said, but enough to confuse the man with the gun.

"Your wallet, asshole," he explained.

I spread my arms, not understanding. *"Nye poni-mayou,"* I said. I don't understand.

It stirred him to new feats of translation. "Listen, prick," he said, and waved the gun. It gave me my first good look at it, and I could see it was plastic, a superb likeness of a Colt .45.

"You won't get far with that thing, sport," I said. "If you're going to be a mugger, you need the real thing. Now, why don't you run away before one of the ladies stuffs that toy gun up your nose?"

He stiffened and glanced down at his gun. I batted it aside and shoved him against another car, pinning him there while I ripped the mask off him and took a look at his face. "Go home," I said. "You're in the wrong line of business."

Then Janet laughed. "I know you," she said. "You played Alec in *The Price of Strawberries* on radio last fall."

Amy joined in her laughter. "Really, John. Did you and Eric cook this up to impress me?"

"Not me," I said. "But since you raise the question . . ." I grabbed the man by the arm and spun him around against the car, where he couldn't get lucky with a wild kick. "Who sent you?"

"My agent," he said through clenched teeth. "I'm sorry. Don't call the police, please. It was supposed to be a joke. I wasn't going to take anything. You can ask her. She told me it was for an audition."

"Who's your agent?" Janet asked.

"Molly Rosewood. Ask her yourself."

"I will," Janet said. "And I'll make sure we never use you again in any production I work on."

I let go of his arm, and he turned, rubbing his wrist, frowning. He was short and seemed shrunken now, the way actors do if you visit backstage and find them taking off their makeup. "I'm sorry. Please. Don't tell anybody. I thought this was legit, an audition."

"I'll think about it," Janet said sternly.

We all stood and looked at him while he picked up his toy gun and backed off, not sure how to make the best exit. I ushered the women into the car. Peter got in next to me in front. The actor watched from the elevator, looking foolish, dropping his eyes as we drove by.

Amy Roger spoke first. "Russian," she said with amusement. "What a good idea. You really put him off his stride."

Like a good courtesan I batted the conversational ball back to her. "You speak Russian? Latin and the Romance languages, I would have thought. Why Russian?"

"I was interested in the early Romanovs," she said easily. "But the academic world is enormously political. To research Peter the Great would have meant trips to Leningrad. That could have been arranged easily enough, but my tutors were all Brits with leftist sympathies. They would have expected a 'What about the workers?' slant to my findings. I might have ended up agreeing with them, but in the meantime there was no room for any subjectivity on my part. Anyway, I did take a year of Russian."

"I suppose you learned yours in the army," Harrod said. He sounded disapproving.

"You have a lot of time to yourself on some assignments," I said. "I used mine in various ways. Did a lot of reading, of course, but also learned a few oddments. One particular time I was isolated with an intelligence officer, and he taught me some rudimentary Russian."

Harrod saw his opportunity and dived in with the obvious "That comes under the heading of an oxymoron, you know. Military intelligence, like airline food. Not possible." He chuckled, but nobody joined him, and he subsided sulkily.

There was nobody in the security office when we drove by. Wainwright was a big tipper, I guessed. But the door had opened up automatically, as he had promised, and we rolled out into the late-evening traffic. "Where are we going?" I asked.

"Three twenty-seven Huron Street," Peter said, then swiveled his head in surprise when Amy asked me, "Are you going through Rosedale?"

"Can do. We're heading north, to Moore Park."

"Oh, fine, then perhaps you could drop me at sixteen Crescent Road," she said. Harrod made an angry humphing noise and sat up very straight in his seat, his arms folded tightly across his chest. Once again the best planned lays of mice an' men had gang agley, I guessed.

He was polite when we dropped him, leaning down to say good night to each of us in a cut-glass voice. I glanced in my mirror as I drove away under a streetlight, but Amy's face was showing nothing I could detect. A cool customer, I thought, perhaps one of those women who liked to tease, giving a suggestion of untold delights and then airily saying good night and vanishing. No wonder the Corsican had got mad at her.

Janet was doing some homework for me. She had been a researcher before she was a producer on her radio show, and she's good at digging out facts. "Is Peter an associate?"

"No. As you heard, his field is the Thirty Years' War," Amy said. "I bump into him in the library all the time, but he's heading off to Prague this summer. I'm going to France."

I decided it was time to talk shop. "I guess you know why Eric brought us together this evening?"

"Eric can be tiresome," she said. "I happened to mention

what happened last summer, and he insists I need someone to look after me."

"And what did happen?" I asked as I turned along Davenport and headed back toward Rosedale.

"Some man got unpleasant, and I looked after myself," she said.

"And you heard what happened to the man on the film crew that night?"

"That was the end of it," she said. "The machismo factor was resolved, and everything went back to normal."

"You know Corsicans better than that," I said.

"What do you know about Corsicans that should color my thinking?" Her voice was cool.

"I once had occasion to escort a British national out of Marseilles. It was a government operation, so I'm not going into any details, but I gave the queen good value for her shilling that day against some highly organized Corsican resistance."

If Amy was impressed, she covered it well. "I don't like the way you and Eric concocted this ridiculous business in the garage," she said angrily. "What was my reaction supposed to be? Was I supposed to blurt out, 'My hero,' shoulder Janet aside, and fall into your arms?"

"Talk to Eric about that one. It was nothing to do with me."

"All right, I will." Her tone was bitter, but there was fear underlying it. She covered it by asking another question. "And suppose you tell me what you would have done if the threat had been real instead of staged."

"I would have kept you safe. It's what I do."

"How?" she sneered. "Would you have told him about your service record?"

"I would have shot him if it was necessary."

She gasped, and Janet spoke. "John is very good, Amy," she said. "He was in the Special Air Service in Britain. He's good. I was in a bad situation once, and he helped me. If someone is trying to hurt you, John can keep you safe."

"I wouldn't expect you to say anything else," Amy said softly.

Janet chuckled. "I don't know how to reply to that one. We're neighbors and friends, nothing more."

Now Amy leaned forward in her seat and snorted. "How does that make you feel, Mr. Locke? Your smoke screen just blew away."

"Be as bitchy as you like to me, Amy," I said pleasantly. "But Janet is my friend, and I'd like you better if you treated her with courtesy. Now, if you'll give me some directions, we'll bring this unpleasant evening to an end."

"Turn left at Crescent Road," she said quietly, then added, "Please," and sat back.

Nobody said anything else as I drove to her door and stopped. She was out of the car immediately, but I got out and watched until she reached the door. Then she turned and called, "Thank you for the ride home. Good night."

I raised my hand to her and got back into the car as the light went on in the hall. "Thank the Lord that's over," I said to Janet. "Would you like to come up front for the last leg?"

"Yes," she said. She changed seats, and I caught the faint perfume of her hair. Impulsively, I reached over and kissed her cheek. "Thanks for the character reference."

"Thanks for making gentlemanly noises," she said. "That lady has a wide streak of rich bitch in her makeup."

"It doesn't matter, anyway. She won't want me along."

Janet turned her head toward me and put her hand on

my arm. "Just watch yourself if you do get the job," she said.

We exchanged pecks at her door, and I went up to my place. There was one phone message. It was Wainwright. His voice was cold. "Wainwright here. Call me when you get in." He was cracking the five-thousand-dollar whip he had bought that morning.

I called, and he picked it up first bounce.

"Locke here, returning your call." I could be laconic myself.

"What went wrong?" he snapped.

"I assume you've already talked to Mickey Mouse."

"What's that supposed to mean?"

"Think hard, Eric. Try and remember the chorus boy you hired to play with guns. Did you really think your niece would buy a charade like that?"

"Now listen." His voice was harsh. "You can't talk to me that way."

"Why not? She's nixed the deal. I'm not working for you anymore. I'll return your deposit tomorrow."

I hung up angrily. Damn his clumsiness. The job was attractive. And so was the very high-handed Amy Roger. Ah well. Back to watching the newspapers. There was a whole summer crop of movies to be shot in Toronto. Somebody out there would want my services.

It must have been five minutes later that the phone rang again.

"John Locke."

"Did you have a gun with you tonight?" It was Amy.

"Yes." I left it crisp. She had the apologizing to do, not me.

"I didn't notice anything."

"You weren't supposed to."

She hesitated; her words were spaced and ragged as she put her question together. "Have you ever used it?"

"On a number of occasions. I'm very good." The truth is not a boast, my father says. If you can do this job, say so.

"I've been reading since I came in," she said. "The Special Air Service is the group that entered the Iranian embassy in London when they had that hostage incident."

"I was part of that team." It was the only time the SAS conducted a maneuver in full view of the media. Terrorist activity in Britain has diminished since then.

Her voice was harsh when she spoke again. Apologies do not come easily to women like her. "I'm sorry I spoke the way I did, especially if I offended your friend."

"She doesn't hold grudges. Neither do I. You're under more stress than you're admitting, even to yourself." A good line, I thought. I wasn't going to plead for the job. If a hint didn't do it, the hell with it.

"Then I'd like to take advantage of Eric's offer," she said. "Can we talk about it tomorrow, perhaps?"

"How about lunch?"

"I'll be free about one o'clock."

"Good. Shall I pick you up somewhere?"

"How about in front of the reference library on Yonge Street. You know where it is?"

It was time to acknowledge the importance I put on this job. "I spent today there reading your thesis."

She laughed. "You're very professional, John. I think I'll enjoy having you along," she said. "One o'clock, then."

"One o'clock. Good night." I waited for her to hang up and then did the same, smiling. I was going back to France, after all.

CHAPTER

4

THE NEXT couple of days went fast. I used them well. First thing I did was to warm up the contacts I'd made with the security forces of France and Canada back when I was with the SAS full-time. Through a friend who's the boss of security at Toronto airport I was able to get the pass I needed to wear my gun while boarding. I could have smuggled it through in the bag I checked, but there was the outside chance it would miss the flight and end up in Addis Ababa.

A phone call to Claude Fussel of Interpol in Paris got me the same permits at his end, and I was able to travel armed, prepared for trouble.

I also spent a beery evening with Martin Cahill, a good buddy of mine who is an inspector with the RCMP, the Mounties. He's involved with the dope squad and has access to all the information they hold on organized crime worldwide. I wanted to know what he could tell me about the Corsicans, specifically Vittore Orsini, the guy who was making my trip necessary.

Martin brought me a photograph. "It's fifteen years old," he apologized. "That was the last time he was arrested, murder. He got off, of course. The key witness lost his memory."

I checked it over. Orsini looked tough. According to the details on the back of the photograph, he had been forty-nine at the time. He was 168 centimeters tall, around five feet six, and had a couple of interesting scars—knife and bullet wounds. The photo showed me that he was a solid-shouldered guy, the fisherman type, arms knotted up with muscle from hauling nets. He had a full head of black hair, graying handsomely at the temples, and a full mustache. His face had that flat, expressionless quality you see in a lot of criminals, especially those who've done heavy time inside. According to the file he hadn't, but Martin gave me some details that explained the look.

"Interesting guy," he said. "Born in Corsica, grew up in Marseilles. In 1942 he was seventeen. That was when the Germans took over all of France, not just the north, which they occupied in 1940, after Dunkirk. Seems his family owned a bar in the dock area. Anyway, some German soldier got rough with Orsini's sister. Could have been a rape, could've been just that he groped her. Anyway, it was enough to get Vittore fired up, and he cut the guy's throat."

"Then what? Did the Germans shoot a bunch of hostages?" That was their usual tactic, courtesy of Clausewitz, their high priest of total war.

Martin nodded, creasing his big Irish face into a frown. "They did, and they also put a price on the kid's head. So he dropped out of sight. Nothing more about him on the record until after the war."

"Then what? Did he cut more throats?"

"For a while." Martin took a pull at the glass of Bushmills I'd poured him. "Things were pretty hectic at that time. The civil authorities were in disorder, food was short, and there were still some German troops around, trying to get back home. The authorities didn't know how to handle things. I don't have any details. However, they do know that Orsini drifted into the black-market rackets, and when things improved, he went from that into rackets, period. He's the godfather to a whole Marseilles family."

"What kind of stuff are they into? The same as the mobs over here?" I expected the worst. Gangsters are gangsters in any culture, but I could almost empathize with Orsini. Maybe he would have grown up to be a hood anyway, but there was an outside chance that he was just another war casualty, a man whose life had been altered totally by the experiences he'd had as a young guy in an occupied country.

" 'Bout the same," Martin said. "Protection, girls, dope. Dope's big, of course. I guess you know that Marseilles is on the pipeline from Thailand into the States and Canada."

"I saw *The French Connection*."

"Yeah, well, the guy with the beard could've been Orsini."

That was about all the hard information he had for me. I took a long last look at the photograph, committing Orsini's face to memory, trying to work out what he would look like now. Martin solved that problem for me. "We've got a computer program at the office; it shows us what age will do to a guy's face. I've already asked the operator to work on this one, and I'll have a computer likeness for you by tomorrow."

"Thanks. I don't want to have to wait for this girl to remember whether it's him or not. That's liable to take too long if Orsini shows up."

"Tomorrow," he said. "Which reminds me, I've gotta

be back in the office at seven. I'm for bed. You wanna crash on the couch?"

"Naah, I'll head home." I stood up. "Thanks for the help, Martin. Okay if I call you if I run into some questions over there?

"Always happy to oblige a taxpayer," he said, "'specially when he's just bought me a jug of Bushmills. Thanks, buddy." I gave him a thumbs up and left.

I picked up the photograph next day. Two of them, in fact; one eight by ten, the other a reduction to wallet size. It was a remarkable job. The computer had shown the sagging of age and the lines that would have developed, based on the original round, hard structure of Orsini's skull. He still looked tough, but now it seemed that he was more vulnerable, more likely to delegate any rough stuff. It made me conscious that I would have to earn my keep on this trip. Anybody from outside the community we were staying in could be one of Orsini's men.

We flew out of Toronto the following Wednesday night, first-class on Air France, courtesy of Wainwright. It's the civilized way to travel, and I enjoyed it. Amy looked delicious. She had made it clear by her attitude that I was the hired help and had better not write any scenarios containing clinches. That didn't stop the attendants from drawing the obvious conclusion when they saw us traveling together, and they poured the champagne as if it were our wedding night. Surprisingly, Amy had a head for it and socked back three glasses before saying no. After an excellent dinner we both slept and woke up to coffee and croissants before landing at Charles de Gaulle Airport around nine.

It's ultramodern, built like a set for *2001*, with interconnecting glass tubes containing the escalators. But it's not all show. The French are very businesslike, and security is tight.

Amy went ahead of me in the line and had to explain all about her archaeological chores and listen to a stern warning not to export any antiquities. My French isn't bad, but hers left me for dead. She rattled at the guy just as rapidly as he did to her. I decided to let her do the bargaining for us if I wanted to bring back a souvenir. Finally, she was through and stood waiting for me.

I preempted any problems for myself by showing my Interpol pass at Immigration and was waved through, much to Amy's annoyance.

"How come you rated the VIP treatment?" she wanted to know as she picked up her carry-on bag.

"Friends in high places," I said.

We had time for a café au lait and then took our flight to Lyons. "That's another thing," she grumbled as we lined up for the flight. "Why did you insist on coming through Lyons? Marseilles is an hour closer to Vaison."

"It's also Orsini's hometown," I reminded her. "If he's serious about getting even, he's probably got somebody paid to check the passenger lists."

She tossed her head impatiently. "And just how is he to know I'm coming back?"

"Remember that Corsica invented the vendetta. If this particular Corsican is serious, he's likely found out everything there is to know about you, including the fact that you're working on a thesis. He knows you'll come back, and he wants to know when you'll get here."

She paused to hand in her boarding pass, beaming at the girl who took it, then turning to frown at me. "If you ask me, it sounds like you're dressing this incident up so that you can inflate your paycheck."

"Thanks for the vote of confidence," I said. I didn't bother arguing. One of the maxims in the SAS is train hard, fight easy. That's the way I still work, regardless of client comment.

We took our seats, and I pulled out the eight by ten Martin had given me. "Is this your man?"

She took it, surprised. "Where did this come from?"

"Is it Orsini?" I can be high-handed, too.

"His mustache is dark, not grizzled, but otherwise yes," she said. "But where did you get it? I know Eric was trying to find a picture and had no luck. And he's got friends all over the place."

"So do I," I said. Advantage Locke. I made a note to tell Martin that his computer guy did neat work.

We picked up our hire car from Hertz, a neat Ford Sierra, a British car, but with left-hand drive. From the airport we drove out ot the Périphérique, the road that encircles Lyons, paying six francs for the privilege, and then headed south on to the Autoroute. Just outside the city we stopped and picked up our ticket at the *péage* booth, and I wound the car up to a smooth 140 K, about 85 miles per hour. It was pleasant. The road was busy with vacationers. Maybe a third of France takes holidays in July—the rest do it in August but most of the cars were driving slower than me, and I was able to cruise comfortably. The scenery was interesting. The land is cultivated but dry and rugged, much like Tuscany. The sun was already high, and the temperature was in the low thirties, pushing ninety on the old Fahrenheit scale.

Amy slept until we left the highway at Bollène, paying forty francs, about seven American dollars, for our two hundred k of highway. And then we were out into Provence proper. The road winds through vineyards and little villages of the local yellow stone with orange tile roofs, most of them sun-bleached with age down to a soft umber.

"You know how to get to Vaison?" she asked.

"I've checked the map. Are we going right there?"

"First," she said, "I want to talk to my contact in town before I go on to Faucon."

"Who are you seeing, the local director of antiquities?"

"No," she said tersely.

I glanced over at her. "Sorry if I stepped on a corn. I figured there'd be somebody in charge of history there, that's all."

"There is, but I'm not working on the Romans this time."

I mouthed an "Oh." There's enough history in the region to keep an army busy for a lifetime. The place has been inhabited virtually forever and been farmed for close to two thousand years. When she volunteered nothing, I prodded a little. "I'm not about to pirate your work, Amy. It might help me do my job if I knew your plans, that's all."

"I don't see how," she said tartly.

"It will give me a general idea of what the people you know and trust will look like," I said. "If you're researching the Benedictines, I'll know that priests are going to be in and out of your life. If it's Roman history, I'll expect scholarly-looking people with small hands and feet. That kind of thing."

She relaxed a little. "Okay, I see what you mean. "Well, I'm working on something different."

"World War II," I ventured.

She gave a little gasp of surprise. "What makes you say that?"

"You didn't respond to Benedectines, and you're not doing the Romans this time. I made the natural assumption."

She turned her face away, staring down the road at the endless grapevines on either side. "Why would you assume that?"

"This place has been a backwater for the last five hundred years." I was glad of the chance to air a little knowledge of my own. "They're largely Catholic still. The Reformation didn't make much headway down here. The Franco-Prussian War didn't affect them as it did the north. Nor did the First World War. That leaves the Second. They were occupied, and a few places had a hard time, but not Vaison."

"There are some people here who have information I want," she said. "It's the kind of stuff you have to dig for. People don't volunteer it. I have to spend time with them, earn their trust."

I didn't say anything, but I wondered why she had chosen Provence as a research project. To the best of my knowledge, war activity in the area had consisted of sporadic attacks on German installations, sabotage of trains and supplies. And very few people had been involved. Even as late as 1945 most French people were passive toward the Germans. They're republican, often anti-American, but they have lots of rightists there, and they liked the law and order that Hitler provided. The Maquis had been a very small group, consisting for the most part of Communists plus a few hotheads like Vittore Orsini. Now, forty-five years later, everyone old enough claims to have been a Resistance fighter. But even the president's credentials have been questioned. Amy would have to be half detective, half diplomat if she was going to find any facts.

"So you'll be dealing mostly with elderly people?" I suggested.

"Yes," she said, and shut up until we reached Vaison-la-Romaine.

We drove up the rising road past the cathedral and pulled into the main square, the Place de Montfort. It's what people imagine when they picture rural France. There's a row of bistros down one side, sheltered by plane trees that have been cut back over the years until they resemble over-sized bonsai. In the center of the square is an open area, used as a parking lot except on Tuesdays—market days—when it fills up with stalls. There's a moss-covered fountain in it and trees of its own. At Amy's suggestion I parked under one of them and locked the car; then we sauntered across to Le Siècle, one of the busier restaurants.

We sat outside under an awning, and a waiter bustled up wearing a shirt with tricolor decorations. Amy studied the shirt as she ordered a café au lait for us.

"You forgot the Revolution in your vest-pocket history of the region," she said dryly.

"Yes, I know this is the bicentennial year, but again, it didn't hit this region in any special way."

She looked amused. "Not just a pretty face, are you?"

"Not even," I responded automatically. She was studying me, and I did the same with her. Here, in a French café where all the girls were chic and interesting looking, even the plain ones, she was not such a standout as she had seemed in Toronto. But she had an intelligence in her eyes that made her beauty remarkable. I'm the typical male chauv, but I like bright women, and I liked her. Maybe things would work out differently from the way she had it planned. Time would tell.

We finished, and I paid for the drinks. "Okay, work time," she said. "Why don't you take a look around? I'll be about half an hour."

"That's not the way it goes," I said politely. "If you're seeing somebody, I'll wait outside the place, but I'm not losing touch with you."

"Oh, brother," she said, but she didn't argue. "Okay, I guess that makes sense for now. But if I change my mind, I'll let you know."

"If you need to be alone with anybody, you won't even know I'm there," I promised. "I've done a lot of this, including taking care of rock stars and politicians who wanted privacy for their assignations. Don't worry."

She flushed slightly at that, and I wondered whether I'd touched a nerve. Perhaps her contact here was some boyfriend from the previous year.

We took the car and drove up to the Haute-Ville, the old fortified section of the town. The streets are narrow and steep, and not many cars penetrate this high, but we found a parking space in a little open square, and she said, "I'm going to see somebody now, in that house over there."

I glanced at it. It was a row house, one of a street of separate homes side by side in a single building. The one she pointed out had only one door, and I knew that all the houses backed onto a sheer drop down to the river. "Fine. I'll wait," I said.

We got out, and she clipped over the cobblestones on her wooden-soled sandals. I kept her in sight but moved away. There was nobody in the square but the pair of us, and most of the windows were shuttered. Those that were not had nobody at them. If this had been a case of protecting her from an assassin's bullet, I would still have been concerned, but I figured Orsini wanted her very much alive. That meant he was going to have to take her prisoner, and that wasn't going to happen here, not with me on her side and armed.

She tugged the bell pull beside the door, and after a few

seconds a man answered it. He was fortyish and had a pale face and the small-lensed, round spectacles of a scholar. He looked annoyed when he opened the door, but he beamed with delight when he saw her, and they exchanged enthusiastic kisses on the cheek, the three kisses of good friends. He was the reason she had flushed, I guessed.

He invited her in, and I made myself inconspicuous. I'd brought my camera with me, and I made like a tourist, clicking away at the hanging flowerpots and the ancient doorways and a big yellow dog with its left front leg missing. He was lying in the sun like an old war veteran. I clicked my tongue at him, and he opened one eye to look me over, then closed it, uninterested.

Time passed slowly. There wasn't much traffic: a very few pedestrians, women mostly, carrying their shopping bags back from the stores in the town center, and a couple of kids. There was also a tourist couple, honeymooners by the look of them, and a few cars. Most of them drove through in low gear, going slowly over the bumpy stones. But then a Mercedes drew up. It had two men in it in shirtsleeves.

There was plenty of room beside my car, but they parked awkwardly across the street, and they didn't get out. The passenger had a small camera, and he aimed it around the square in a bored fashion, but the only time it clicked was when he had my car in his sights, including the rear license plate. I unzipped the light jacket I was wearing but went on taking pictures. They looked at me without interest, and I moved off, around the first corner, out of their line of sight. I could still see the door Amy had gone through, plus the rear of their car, and I was close enough to hear if their doors opened. Two steps would bring me back into the square if anything changed.

Nothing did for half an hour. Then the house door opened again, and Amy stepped out, the man holding her arm. I heard the snap of a car-door lock, and I took the two steps back into the square, knotting the strap of my camera around my left hand, turning the Pentax into a handy club. My right hand was free, and I reached around and unsnapped the catch of my holster.

The two men were out of the car. Amy was not paying them any heed. She was holding both of the man's hands, and he was gazing into her eyes with what passes for adoration among Frenchmen.

The two men separated and wandered toward Amy, one on each side of her, but there was no menace in their gait, and I noticed that their hands were empty. If they had designs on her, they were to abduct her, not to harm her. Orsini had specified that, I was certain.

I kept coming, strolling as casually as they were, the idle tourist. And then, when I was a dozen yards away, they pounced.

The one on the left moved first. He stepped forward and shoved Amy's friend, sending him sprawling on the cobblestones. The other one grabbed Amy by one hand. It looked amateur, but he was good. He had her in a come-along hold, and all she could do was shriek and go with him, backward, reluctantly, but at the speed he was dictating with the pressure he had on her hand.

I went into my act. "I say," I shouted in an effete English accent, "I say, you. Fellow. Let go of that girl."

The one who had done the shoving turned and grinned at his buddy, almost licking his lips. Then he came at me.

I could tell by his stance that he was a savate expert, a foot boxer, and I knew what to expect. He sprang toward me, but instead of falling into a boxing crouch, as he'd anticipated from my accent, I sprang toward him, too close for the kick he was swinging at my jaw, hinging his leg in from the side. I was against him by then, and I uppercut him straight into his unprotected testicles.

He fell, writhing, clutching his groin, and I came on at the second man. He was smarter. He pulled a knife and held it against Amy's neck, not her throat but the side of her neck. He grinned at me, and I noticed he had a bum eye on the left. It was focused off center, making him look even more menacing. He made a flicking motion with his knife, a signal for me to leave.

Amy was staring at me, her eyes wide, the whites showing. She said nothing, but her fear filled the square. I went back into my act, the concerned tourist. Maybe he would think I'd just been lucky with that punch to his partner's equipment.

"Drop that silly knife," I said angrily. He hissed something and backed up, dragging Amy toward the car. I glanced over my shoulder; his friend was trying to get to his knees. Time was running out. I changed gears, shouting past him in deliberately lousy French. *"Gendarme! Cet homme avez une couteau."*

It worked. He had me figured for a lucky fool, and he glanced over his shoulder. I balled my fist, with the thumb projecting a half inch, and stabbed him in the eye. It was not enough to burst the eyeball, but he screamed and dropped the knife, and I kicked him in the stomach, sending him sprawling. Then I picked up the knife and stabbed it into both rear tires on the Merc.

Amy was standing straddle-legged, speechless. Her friend was picking himself up. "This is terrible," I said to her, still affecting the English accent. *"Habitez-vous ici?"* Do you live here? I winked at her at the same time and indicated the house she had left.

She caught on. *"Oui, m'sieur,"* she said.

"Bonne," I said, then lapsed back into English. "Why don't we all go in there and call the gendarmes?"

Amy's friend was adjusting his glasses. From scholarly pale his complexion had gone almost green. He was terrified but game.

"D'accord," he said, and then rattled off an invitation to us in French too fast for me to follow.

I took one last look around at the two men, who were on their feet now, one holding his eye, the other his testicles.

"We're going in to call the police," I said sternly, and followed the other two into the house.

CHAPTER

5

I STOOD at the door for an extra moment, looking back sternly and wagging my finger at the walking wounded. They didn't meet my stare; they were busy wrapping the last shreds of their machismo around them, trying to rebuild enough confidence to get the hell out of there. The one who had been holding Amy was leaning against the back of the car, covering his injured eye with one hand. The French don't have the same rich heritage of bad language that we do, but he was improvising handily as he straightened up and lurched away. The other one followed as best he could, hunched down over his insulted testicles. He was bent so low he seemed to be walking on his knuckles, like a gorilla.

I closed the door at last, and Amy grabbed me by the lapel. "What kind of stupid game were you playing?"

I ignored the question. "Is there a phone in the house?"

The man answered, "Yes, over there."

"Good. Call the Gendarmerie. If they're quick, they'll get both those guys."

"*D'accord,*" he said, and went to the phone.

Amy gave my jacket another petulant tug. "What were

you doing? Why didn't you just take your gun out and stop them?"

"I stopped them," I said, gently taking her hand off my lapel. "And they still don't know you've got a bodyguard. They think I'm some Brit tourist who got lucky. It gives us another chance before they get wise and start shooting instead of grabbing."

That brought her up short, and she sagged against the table limply, dealing with her fear. I went to the window and looked out. The two men were leaving the square, adjusting painfully to the downgrade. The three-legged dog woofed at them in a neighborly fashion as they passed, a fellow veteran, remembering his own Saint Crispin's Day.

I turned back to Amy. "Does your buddy have any brandy? You could use a drink."

"I'm fine," she said, and then, in a voice that quavered slightly, "Thank you. For what you did out there."

"It's why I'm here," I said. "Only they still don't know it."

Her friend had reached the police desk, and he was describing the guys in the square. I cut in.

"Tell them one was around 160 centimeters, dark blue pants, light blue shirt, black soft shoes, white socks. The other was around 180 centimeters, good build, brown pants, brown shirt. His left eye wanders—it's out of phase with the right—and it's bloodshot and black. He's covering it with his hand."

The Frenchman turned to glance at me in astonishment. He obviously hadn't got anywhere near as good a description. But he passed the information on, and after a minute's worth of talk he covered the phone and gestured for me to take it.

"Captain Labrosse wants to speak to you. He speaks English."

I took the phone. "John Locke here, Captain."

"You stop these men from take the girl?" His voice was as blunt as his English. He sounded like one of the tough old paras who fought dirty in Algeria. I decided it would be a dumb idea to get on the bad side of this guy.

"I was very lucky, Captain. And by the way, they came in a car, a Mercedes sedan, license number 100 JT 13. It's outside; the tires went flat."

"One wonders how this 'appen," he said dryly.

"One of the men had a knife. It must have cut the tires."

"Good," he said. "That is a Marseilles license. I must check who owns this car, M'sieur Locke. You will remain where you are, please."

"*D'accord*, Captain," I said. There! Bilingual.

He hung up, and I followed suit. The other two were watching me silently, still stunned from the activity outside.

I stuck my hand out to the Frenchman. "John Locke," I told him. "I'm here to keep an eye on Amy."

"Pierre Armand." He straightened out of his academic stoop and took my hand.

"If you had some cognac, Pierre, it might help us all to calm down."

"Ah, yes." He slapped his hands together and left the room. I waved Amy to a chair. It didn't look comfortable. Nothing in the room did. It was Pierre's study, a couple of hard chairs, bookshelves, and a table covered with books and documents. A scholar's workplace. I took the other chair.

Pierre came back in a minute or so with cognac. Amy still had not spoken. She was looking down at a spot on the tiled floor in front of her as if the secrets of the future were spelled out in its dull red face. American veterans of Nam call it "the thousand-yard stare." The starer isn't looking out at all; he's looking inward for as far as it goes and realizing that the horizon is a lot closer than he used to think.

Pierre gave us each a cognac, and Amy took a sip of hers. That she'd made the effort meant she was getting over her fright. It was time to talk turkey.

"This is starting to look organized," I told her. "You've only been in the area since noon and they're already on to you. It means Orsini is serious. Are you happy going on, or would you rather go home?"

Pierre said nothing. From the look he gave Amy I figured he had a case on her. He wasn't going to urge her to leave.

She wasn't going, anyway. Her chin was firm, and she set down her glass and stood up. "I'm here to do a job," she said in a flat voice. "With you here I should be able to finish it. Then I'll go home, not before."

"Fine. Just plan on being extra careful and keeping close to me all the time," I said.

Pierre spoke next, nervously. "You are very good, M'sieur Locke. Those men were street fighters, but you hit them first."

"Today," I said. "There's no guarantee they'll be fooled a second time. If they're serious about taking Amy, they might just shoot me."

"Yes . . ." He rubbed his scalp with his left hand. "That thought also came to me," he said. I noticed that his English had a faint London accent.

Amy didn't add anything. She was deep inside herself, trying to get used to the idea of being in real danger. She was quiet but calm; her hands didn't tremble as she sipped her drink again. A strong woman. Or maybe she had been overimpressed by the way I handled things. Perhaps she thought having me along made her totally fireproof. I knew better. Those men hadn't been armed except for the knife, but Orsini probably had a lot more, better-armed guys on his payroll. This was going to be an interesting assignment.

Captain Labrosse arrived a couple of minutes later. He was a smart fiftyish man in uniform, looking as if he had spent his entire life in the service. He was wearing the picture-postcard kepi you see on the Paris police. His tunic had a row of medal ribbons.

"You are M'sieur Locke. The two men you describe. I 'ave them outside, in my car," he said with a touch of pride.

"Well done," I said. "Why doesn't Ma'amselle Roger identify them and charge them with trying to kidnap her?"

"Of course. You stay here. I will talk to you."

That suited me just fine. I figured the two men would have only a vague recollection of how I looked. I didn't want to give them a chance to adjust it.

I watched from the window as he led Amy back outside. The two men were in the back of his car, and a young gendarme was in the front. From the way the men were sitting I could tell they were handcuffed behind their backs.

Amy looked at them both, pointing to the one who had held her. Then she spoke rapidly, and Labrosse nodded. He gave his driver instructions, and the man reached into the car and picked up the radio mike. I noticed that most of the unshuttered windows around the square now had faces at them, women mostly, but a couple of elderly men.

Labrosse ushered Amy back into the house. He came into Pierre's little workroom and looked around it coolly. "Have you a place where we can sit?"

"Mais oui." Pierre ushered us through to the other downstairs room, a nineteenth-century French drawing room filled with heavy, plush furniture and old knicknacks. Labrosse nodded.

"Good. Now, per'aps ma'amselle will tell me what is going on."

Amy spoke in French. I could follow about a third of it. My own French is best delivered at seduction speed, with plenty of long, meaningful pauses while I rake together the vocabulary I need to continue. But I caught the name Orsini, and I saw Labrosse's eyes tighten.

At last he nodded to her and turned to me. "And you are the bodyguard?"

"Right." I pulled out one of my natty blue business cards and gave it to him. He took it and grinned. "If you will forgive my words, M'sieur Locke, you do not look like a bodyguard."

"I'm a master of disguise," I said, and he grinned again.

"And what are your qualifications for this task?"

"Ten years in the British army, including seven in the SAS."

That whisked the grin off his face. "The SAS. *Formidable!*"

There's no need to add anything to that, so I asked, "What are you planning to do with the two guys in the car, Captain?"

"They will be charged with assault." He shrugged. "If they choose to tell me why they were 'ere, *bien*. If not." He shrugged again, that wonderful dismissive gesture.

"And what about Miss Roger? Will she have to appear in court?"

"This causes you concern?"

"Some," I said. "If their boss knows Amy's going to be

in court, he will probably plan to follow her from there."

He glared at me. "You want me to release these men? You think this will keep her safe?"

"Miss Roger is going to be here for a few weeks only," I said. "If you could lock them up and set a trial date for, let's say, September, then she would be gone. The case would be thrown out, but she would be safe."

"You ask much," he said. "But I will try to do this."

He turned back to Amy. She had composed herself totally by now. She was tired from the all-night flight, and the attack had drained her, but she was calm, and in this museum setting she looked very beautiful. "What is the nature of your business here, ma'amselle?"

"I'm a historian, working on a paper. I have people to see here."

Labrosse frowned. "And this paper, with what does it deal?"

"As a matter of fact, you're one of the people I want to talk to, Captain," she said. "My subject is the Resistance."

Lord! They're born with style, the French. He cocked one eyebrow and asked, "And just 'ow old do you think I am, ma'amselle?"

"Old enough to have run errands for them as a child. And I know your father was murdered by the Germans." She was regaining her confidence as she talked, getting back into her professional mode. "I know that it cost him his life. He was a brave man."

"Thank you," he said. "You may expect me to cooperate in any way possible." His English was improving with every sentence. It was like watching a rusty old machine start pumping, settling into the rhythm until the clunking becomes almost music. He didn't even pause for her response. "Of course, in the days, duty," he said, and shrugged. He had a cozy tête-à-tête dinner on his mind.

"Some evening, at your convenience, Captain," Amy said. She was aware she was getting the treatment, but she acted calmly. She would handle him as she considered fit. Pierre was listening to the exchange anxiously. Jealousy came off him in waves. I was calmer. Amy's evening with Labrosse would be an evening off. He was quite capable of guarding Amy's body.

The doorbell rang, and Pierre answered it. I listened to the exchange, getting the drift about half a beat later than Labrosse. "My car," he said. He stood up and gave Amy a neat military salute. "Ma'amselle. I will await your pleasure."

"Thank you, Captain. And thank you for your speed today." She could dispense the snake oil just as smoothly as he.

He gave me a brisk little nod and marched out. I followed to the outer room and watched as he ordered his driver to accompany the other man with the prisoners; then he paused to light a Gauloise and got into the new car, turning crisply and spurting away through the archway.

Amy was standing beside me. "Well, it's an ill wind," I said.

"Yes," she said, the hint of a satisfied smile on her lips. Labrosse had made his impression.

She said her good-byes to Pierre, I retrieved my camera, and we left. "Where now?" I asked.

"Faucon. It's a couple of miles out of town." She sat back in her seat, totally relaxed. The cognac and Labrosse's professionalism had restored her confidence. I've seen it happen before. In another day my rescue would be forgotten totally. She would remember only the clumsiness I'd adapted. If nobody else took a stab at kidnapping her, she would laugh about me in the fall, around the faculty coffee table, five thousand miles from harm. It didn't rankle. I was getting paid for protecting her, not for making my presence obvious. It's the story that's important, not the words.

Faucon is a typical Provençal village. It was walled once, a couple of hundred years back, and the wall still stands, although these days there are houses outside it. The village sits on a small hill. Vineyards stretch out on all sides until they run into land too rough for cultivation. That's a rarity in France. They have more land under the plough than the whole of Canada, but here you see copses of oaks and pines growing up the side of the hills. This is where the Resistance hid, playing peekaboo with the might of the German army.

"Drive on down the slope," she commanded, and we passed the ELF gas station, with its bar and *pétanque* court, roasting gently under the midmorning sun. Then we drove by a gorge on the left side and came to a small hand-painted sign: La Fongeline. "Down there," she told me, and I turned off.

The path dropped steeply, and I hooked the gear into low, turning with the path that led downward, along the side of a steep drop. "This used to be the main coach road to Marseilles," Amy said. Her voice had the dreamy quality of someone who lives history. Right now she was sharing the excitement and discomfort of those sweating coach passengers of a century before. We passed a small abandoned house, and she waved at it casually. "That was a Benedectine abbey in the thirteenth century." I didn't answer, not wanting to intrude on the pleasure of her thoughts. Then she told me, "Turn right at the bottom."

I did and bumped up an even narrower track between

overhanging trees. "This place is a truffle farm," she explained. "But Madame is not your average farmer. She has a Ph.D. from Columbia, speaks eight languages. Her bookshelf is something to see."

I nodded and concentrated on trying to avoid bottoming the springs in the ruts, turning one last corner and coming up past a carefully planted grove of young oak trees to a fine old stone house. A tiny, gnomelike person, smoking a pipe, was cutting the grass with a whipper-snipper. I was surprised to see it was a very old woman. She stopped the machine when she saw us and came over to the track. I stopped the car, and we got out.

"Amy," the old woman said, and they embraced and exchanged kisses on the cheek.

"This is John Locke," Amy said, and added something in French. "John, this is Constance."

"I assumed he was a husband, not a bodyguard." Constance smiled at me, showing teeth that were large and gappy but all there, not a bad accomplishment for someone as old as she obviously was. She reached up and shook my hand. Hers was tiny but hard. "Do I call you Mr. Locke or John?"

"John, I hope. And do I call you Constance?"

"Ah, that name. 'A poor thing but mine own,'" she said, cocking her head like a little bird.

I know a challenge when I see one. "I think Shakespeare said 'ill-favour'd.'"

Now she inclined her head slowly. "Very good." She turned to Amy. "He has read a book, this bodyguard of yours."

Amy said nothing, but she was looking at me with something like respect. She probably thought I knew my way around Shakespeare. I don't, but I was shut up in a British army Belfast strongpoint for a month once with nothing to read but *Bartlett's Familiar Quotations*. It's the *Reader's Digest* way to look well-read.

I went back to the car, trailing clouds of glory, and drove around and parked, facing back the way we had come, ready to roll in a hurry if necessary. I glanced around at the terrain. It was not good for defense. Immediately behind the house there was a steep rise that led up into trees at the top. A company of troops could creep up without being seen and come down on the house like a plague of locusts before I could do anything about it.

The women joined me as I got the bags out of the car. Amy had her duty-free bag separate, and she handed it to Constance. The old woman pulled out the liter of Scotch it contained and beamed. "How thoughtful. Thank you, my dear." Not your standard grandmother. I was going to like her a lot.

She offered refreshments, but Amy said no. She wanted to rest, so Constance showed us up to the apartment she rented out. It had a kitchen, a bathroom, and a long sitting room filled with hard, old furniture. From the kitchen a short staircase without banisters led up to two bedrooms. One was small; I drew that one. The other was huge but had a low ceiling and one small window. Already the room was filling up with the afternoon heat. It faced west, and I knew it would be stifling by bedtime.

Amy took that one; it had a closet. "I'm going to shower, then sleep," she said. "How about you?"

"You first." I waved her on, and she made for the bathroom, grabbing a towel as she went. There was a bottle of water in the little refrigerator, and I poured myself a large glass and sat on the hard couch and waited. After ten minutes, Amy emerged, wearing a housecoat, her hair wrapped in the towel. "That's better," she said cheerfully. She might have been any tourist with nothing to fear from Orsini or anybody else.

"Go ahead and snooze," I said. "And when you're rested, maybe we can make plans."

"Okay." She nodded and went upstairs. That's when a woman's figure shows to advantage, and with the light housecoat tugged tightly around her, she was a pleasure to watch. I locked the outer door and ducked into the shower, taking my gun into the bathroom with me and leaving the curtain open so I could hear any uproar outside. There was none, and by the time I got upstairs and peeked in at Amy, she was asleep.

I left her door and mine open and lay down, fully dressed. The siesta hour is a good time for ambushes. I slept lightly but was awake an hour later, before Amy was moving, and went down to the living room. From the window I could see Constance moving among her oaks in front of the house. She had a nondescript dog on a leash, her truffle dog, I imagined, on his summer vacation while the truffles ripened around the roots of the oaks.

Looking out at the trees reminded me that I had been too tired to scout the land properly when we arrived, and I slipped out, locking the front door, and went down into the old tile-roofed drive-shed, what they would have called a carport if they'd had cars in the eighteenth century, where Constance kept her little puddle-jumper car, a Citroën CV.

I was working now, and I noted every entrance to the house. The side door to Constance's quarters led down from the shed, and there was one window where I guessed the sink would be in her kitchen.

On the east side the house was blind except for two small windows, both shut tightly. On the south side was a door that looked as if it hadn't been opened since the last occupant went out to his own funeral. And on the west side, under Amy's window, there was a courtyard with a couple of garden chairs and a big old brass water faucet over a stone sink. There were French doors into what I judged to be Constance's living quarters and a couple of low doorways into outdoor storage spaces.

The only ray of sunshine was Constance's truffle dog. With any luck at all he would be a pathological barker.

Constance saw me as she came back through her trees, puffing on her pipe. She waved, and I walked out to join her. "You approve of my house?" she asked dryly.

"Not the most defensible place I've been in, but it's certainly beautiful."

She gestured casually with her pipe. "We managed. Last year, after Orsini became angry with Amy."

"How many people did you use?"

She shrugged. "All those I could find from the old days. Six, including me."

She included herself without any false pride. She had used a gun before then, her attitude said. It was what one did under provocation.

"You had them where?"

"Where would you have placed them, John?" she asked teasingly. Her voice had become playful, and I could imagine her, forty-five years younger, flirting with my father when he was a young officer with the Canadian army, fighting his way across France.

I turned and pointed where I'd place the men. "One on the hill behind the house. One by the woodpile on the north side, one lower down here, where the path turns. One in the courtyard, one on the south side, and the last one in the living room of Amy's apartment."

"What about the east side?" she asked dryly.

"I figured Bonzo here would take care of that."

She smiled, showing those terrible teeth. "You have done this before."

"Lots of times," I said. "Did Amy tell you she was attacked this morning in Vaison?"

"Yes." She frowned, puffing smoke. "That gives me concern. It says not only that Orsini is serious but that he has good intelligence."

"It bothers me as well. I wonder how he found out so quickly that she was in town."

"Did you stop anywhere before you went to see Pierre Armand?"

"At Le Siècle, for a café au lait. There was hardly time for men to drive from Marseilles even if she had been recognized at once."

"Then the information must have come earlier. Perhaps Orsini has a contact with the airline, someone who would see the passenger lists from Paris."

"It sure looks that way," I said. "This could be an interesting few weeks.

"Well, you know what the Chinese say?" She was testing me again.

" 'May you live long in interesting times.' I'd heard that was more of a curse than a blessing."

She laughed. "Perhaps, but consider the alternative." She stooped and let her dog off the leash. It bounded away to the far side of her grove of oaks and squatted. "Well trained," she said with a twinkle.

She recalled the dog and led it around to the back of the house and tied it up. "Amy is sleeping?"

"Yes. I should get back. I just wanted to assess the house."

"Of course. Perhaps now, when she wakes, you will join me for a drink. We can talk more."

"Thank you. I'd like that." We walked around to the back entrance. She went down her two steps; and I went up. The door was locked, as I'd left it, and I let myself in. Amy was sitting in the living room with a glass of water.

"Sleep well?" I asked her.

"Yes. I find jet lag isn't much of a problem." She spoke with the confidence of someone who habitually travels first-class. I'd found it different in the belly of a Hercules transport back to Britain from the Falklands.

"We should talk," I said. "They're on to you. And from the speed they're moving they've been lying in wait for a year, so they're serious."

Her face became set, a stubborn child. "You can take care of me. You proved that this morning."

"You can count on me to do my best, and that's pretty good. But you have to remember that even the president of the United States isn't safe behind a full corps of body-guards," I said. "I just want you to know that the risk continues."

"You're telling me you're scared?" Her voice was almost sneering, and her pretty face wasn't pretty at that moment.

"I've been in worse situations. I doubt that you have," I said levelly. "It just seems to me that you're taking an academic exercise very seriously, putting it ahead of your own safety."

"You publish or perish in my field." Her voice was crisp, as if she were lecturing her nice, harmless group of students back in Toronto. "I've got a head start on my career with my doctoral paper. Now I've changed focus, and when this assignment is completed, I'll be set for tenure at the U. of

T. and also most likely have a popular audience for my work. This is important."

I raised both hands. "Count on me. Now, why don't you fill me in on who you're going to see?"

"Is that necessary?" The same pouty look.

"I can give you some advice on how to stay safe," I said patiently. "For instance, don't tell anybody who else you're going to see. If they suggest someone, don't tell them when you'll be making the call."

She looked at me without speaking for about half a minute. Then she nodded, a gesture more to herself than to me. Her purse was sitting by the chair, a big straw basket with some cloth label on one side in French. It looked as if she had bought it on her last trip here. She reached in and took out a file and, surprisingly, a pair of reading glasses. I could see through them that her cheek looked smaller. She was myopic.

"Do you want to write these names down?" she asked.

"How nearsighted are you?" I interrupted.

"Normally I wear contacts," she said. "I won't miss anything, if that's what's worrying you."

"If not, wear your glasses," I told her. "You might recognize someone important."

She pursed her lip, biting off some snappish reply. "I've seen this man only once. He looks like that photograph you showed me, so you'll recognize him as quickly as I do."

"Was there anyone else around him?"

"His date, girlfriend, whatever."

"I doubt that she's a permanent fixture, but what did she look like?"

"Like a hooker," she said grimly. "Long hair, long eyelashes, long fingernails."

"Blond, dark? How old? Did she resemble anybody, an actress or someone I'd know?"

The questions made her realize this wasn't a game. She frowned and remembered. "About twenty-five, I'd say. Jet black, dyed hair, pouty, like Bardot."

"That's good. How tall?"

"Five three, but she wore enormous heels, and with her hair puffed up, she was taller than he was."

That was unusual. It suggested Orsini was a confident guy. Most men pick out shorter girls. "Okay. I think I've got her pegged. Did you see anyone else, his chauffeur or someone who might have been a bodyguard?"

"If he had anyone like that along, they stayed outside. I didn't see anybody but people I guessed were film people, you know, casually dressed."

"To be on the safe side, if you recognize any of them, tell me. They might be on his payroll."

She nodded and unfolded her piece of paper. "All right. I'll do that. Now, do you want these names?"

"No. I won't write them down; I'll learn them." I was trained not to put things on paper unnecessarily, but Amy still frowned at me, the theatrical smile, playing to an invisible audience, showing that she was superior to me and my strange ways.

"Where does Pierre fit in? His name isn't on the list."

"He's a friend from Cambridge, a classicist. He was useful on my last assignment, and he might be useful here. I looked him up to see if he can help." Her tone was defensive. She and Pierre had been close at one time, I judged.

"And can he be?"

"He has promised to talk to his own contacts in the

community. He's well known locally; he's lived here since university."

"Doing what?"

"Really," she snapped. "What has this got to do with your guarding me?"

"Did he know you were coming to town today?"

She stood up angrily. "Are you saying he told someone and Orsini heard?"

"Somebody did. And the guys knew exactly where you were."

She took a couple of steps, holding her hands away from her sides. "Is this what it comes down to? Everyone I know is a suspect?"

"What does he live on?" I kept my voice calm. She was in danger, and the sooner she realized the fact, the safer she would become.

"Family money. His father has vineyards. Pierre doesn't have to teach, like me."

"And he's working on something about the Romans?"

She turned to stand over me. If I'd been one of her students, I would have known I was going to get a D minus on my assignment. "Just what the hell does a dropout like you know about anything?" she hissed.

"You can't learn if you don't ask questions. What kind of teacher are you, anyway?" I said mildly.

She threw up her hands and sat down. "Your business disgusts me. You poke and pry into everything."

"Think of me as a historian of the ongoing. I won't ask about anything I don't need to know."

"He's working on a history of the false popes," she said finally. "There, satisfied now?"

"Why isn't he over at Avignon? That's where they held court."

"He spent the winter there. Now he's back in his own home doing his writing. Okay?"

"Fine. Thank you."

She sat in silence, and at last I said, "I was talking to Constance. She asked us down for drinks. What do you say?"

"On condition you keep your damn mouth shut," she said.

I stood up. "You're beautiful when you're mad," I told her, and ducked the cushion she flung at me.

Drinks and, later, dinner with Constance were the best part of the day. Amy had been right about her books. She had three walls of her big room covered with them. Everything from Sartre to Surtees to S. J. Perelman. While the women chattered in French, I excused myself and browsed, drink in hand, finally borrowing a history of the Mongols to read while I was there.

After dinner we went back upstairs. I'd locked the door before we left but went in first, anyway, making sure nobody had slipped in ahead of us. If Orsini knew we were in town, he probably knew where we were staying. But there were no prowlers.

Constance had told me that her dog was noisy if anyone came close, but I made a last check outside before coming in. Everything was still, and Amy was already in her room with the door closed when I got back. I drank a last glass of the good water that had come from the spring that fed the tap in the courtyard and then went to bed, leaving a chair under the door handle of the downstairs room.

I've learned to sleep lightly over the years, and I did, waking before dawn, still on Toronto time. I sat and read about Genghis Khan for an hour, then got up and went for a run, down to the roadway and back three times. It was only about six kilometers, but the hill was punishing, and I was sweating hard when I got back. The door was locked, and the leaf I'd slipped between the edge of the door and the jamb was still in place. I'd been happy to see that the dog barked authoritatively every time I came and went from the house, so I knew we were safe. The only thing was, he had disturbed Constance. She came to the side door as I opened it up. She was wrapped in a terry-cloth bathrobe and for once was not wearing her pipe.

She beckoned me. "Come," she commanded, and I followed her as she led me around to her doghouse. The dog leaped up on the end of his chain, and she went up and petted it, talking in soft idiomatic French that left me clueless about what she was saying.

Then she waved to me. "Let him sniff your hand," she said, and I did. She stopped again and spoke to the dog in a loving whisper. This time I caught two of her words. *"Ton ami."* Your friend. Security clearance, La Fongeline style.

"Now he knows you," she said. "If you insist on this dreary North American business of exercising in the mornings, the rest of the world can sleep."

"Thank you." I stooped and fondled the dog, and he relaxed with me as totally as he seemed to with Constance. *"Bon garçon,"* I said, and Constance laughed.

"Would you like some powerful coffee?"

"Please. If you don't mind the way I'm dressed."

She fondled the dog one last time, then stood all the way up, her full four feet eleven. "I spent the whole of 1944 and part of 1945 living with the Maquis," she said proudly. "You are not showing enough flesh to shock me, John."

"Fair enough," I said. "I'd love some coffee, please."

She led me back in and poured us coffees into the wonderful bowls they sometimes use in France. She added hot milk and gave me a croissant. "The breakfast of champions," she said dryly.

I laughed and raised my coffee. *"Salut."* She smiled. I could see she liked having a guy around. It was time to use the advantage. "Tell me, Constance, how safe would you say Amy can be here?"

She looked at me over the brim of her cup. "It's not going to be easy," she said. "Orsini is tough."

"I know that. He's the head of one of the biggest crime families in Marseilles," I said.

She shook her head impatiently. "Tougher than that, John Locke. Most of those guys sit on their fat asses and have other people do the work. Not him. He cuts his own throats. He was in the Maquis for three years. He was a lone-wolf killer. They called him Le Loup."

CHAPTER

6

I WAS THOUGHTFUL as I went back up to the apartment. Constance's information had raised a couple of questions in my mind. First, if Orsini was one of their own, why had her old buddies from the Resistance turned out to defend Amy the night he first gave her a hard time? If they knew his pedigree, they shouldn't have been so ready to shoot him if he'd tried to harm Amy. That's not the way it happens in the IRA, for instance. They will torture or even kill their own members, but they always have some kind of court-martial first. The Maquis did things more casually, it seemed.

My second question was less philosophical. Had one of the local Resistance vets tipped off Orsini that Amy was coming back to town? Some of them must have known. Just where did their loyalties lie, I wondered.

Constance had given me the names of the Resistance people she had called up the year before. I was planning to check them out with Amy, to see if she had contacted any of them ahead of time and let them know she was coming. A long shot, but if we could find out who was for us and who against, it might make my life a little easier in the weeks to come.

I put coffee on and showered. By the time I was out, the coffee aroma had done the things it does in TV commercials, and Amy was in the kitchen, worrying about breakfast.

It seemed she was a morning person. She was bright and cheerful as she poured the coffee and dug into the croissants Constance had given me for our breakfast.

I told her about Orsini, and she paused in mid-bite to consider the news. "Is Constance certain of her facts?" she asked at last. "I've never heard this before."

"You've heard of Le Loup?"

She nodded impatiently. "Of course. He was kind of a loner. From what I've heard, he started out with a group of others, leftists and men trying to avoid being shipped to Germany to work, the usual crowd." She paused to eat some of her croissant, looking thoughtful as she tried to marshal the facts in her memory. "I think it was 1944 that things fell apart. His group was engaged in some kind of operation, and it went sour. The Germans were waiting for them, and they killed them all, wiped them out to the last man, except for Le Loup."

"Was he the leader?"

"No." She shook her head. "He wasn't even Le Loup at that time. It was after that he built his reputation. He specialized in killing sentries."

I studied her face as she talked. Most men would have shown some emotion at the thought, pro and con, either reveling in the idea of the cowboys beating the Indians or else hating the idea of killing. Amy's face was neutral. She was dealing in historical facts. Taxes had been collected. Throats had been cut. It was all the same to her, another fact for filing.

"And I guess the Germans took reprisals on the locals," I said. "For every German killed they would shoot the mayor of the nearest village, plus half a dozen other men taken at random."

"Yes." She nodded. "There's a plaque in the square at Gordes; they shot a group of hostages there, among other places."

"Mostly that system worked," I said. "If you were from the area, you didn't want to see your neighbors shot. But if you were from Corsica, or Marseilles even, that was different. Your war came first, the inhabitants second. I'd imagine Le Loup was not well liked."

She was hardly listening. "If Orsini is Le Loup, I'd love to talk to him," she said.

I kept my cool. "Don't lose sight of who and what he is now," I reminded her. "Charles Manson may have been a cute little kid once, but talking to him didn't do much for Sharon Tate."

She was too excited by the thought to sit still. She got up, carrying her coffee cup, and walked over to the window. "How serious do you think he is about hurting me, really, John?" She flashed me a girlish smile, as if winning my heart would set her free from threats forever. "I can make him famous," she went on. "Le Loup tells the world what it was like to be a lone freedom fighter."

It was time for a little cold water. "He wants to hurt you," I said shortly. "You humiliated him; he will humiliate you. To a man who deals in sex the way McDonald's deals in hamburgers, that means one thing. Do I really need to draw any pictures?"

Her face went white, and she didn't speak for a long time. Finally, she said, "I guess you're right." She went over to the sink and rinsed her coffee cup under the tap, a mechanical gesture, as if normality could wipe out evil possibilities.

I changed the subject. "What's on the agenda today?"

Slowly, she collected herself. "First I want to talk to Pierre. Then we're going to call on Madame Boulanger; she's on the list I gave you. Her husband was killed by the Germans in 1944."

"Was he an active partisan or just an innocent hostage?"

"Let's find out." She had put her coffee cup in the sink and was now running hot water. I added mine, and our plates, and wiped up as she washed. She was very quiet, contemplating the reality I'd handed her. It's not something I do very often to a client, but I'd never had one who had so much trouble understanding why I was there.

She didn't speak again until we were out in the car. By then I had looked it over for additions the manufacturer hadn't included and had done my best to check that no sniper was in the trees, waiting to knock me out and come on down to claim Amy. "We're going to have to find a new place to live," I told her as we bounced back down the narrow pathway to the road. "By tomorrow they could have this lane closed off. If they're that serious, they'll shoot me and grab you as we come out."

I was looking ahead, watching for a face or the glint of a gun muzzle in the bushes on the roadway, but out of the corner of my eye I saw her turn to look at me, openmouthed in horror. "You think they'd go that far?"

"I'm sure of it. We move today."

"I'm on a budget, and I've already paid for the summer." Her voice was petulant.

"Wainwright will pay. I'll put it on my expense sheet for him."

"But I've told my contacts to call me at Constance's," she persisted. Her pout was audible.

"Then you can call in and pick up your messages. One thing's for sure, Amy. You can't afford the risk of going back to that farm."

We broke out of the lane, and I booted the car up the hill and out onto the roadway, relieved but still alert, checking the rear mirror for strange vehicles.

"Where to?" I asked her.

"Pierre's place first, the old town."

"Right." I put my foot down and concentrated on building up my speed through the winding roadway. If anyone chased us out here, they would be familiar with the roads, I had to be able to outrun them if necessary. It was exhilarating. The road twisted and meandered so that thirty miles an hour would have been pushing it. I hit fifty in a few places.

I slowed when we came to the traffic lights at Vaison, and we drove down the main street, through town and over the bridge to the old quarter. Amy still had not spoken as we pulled into the little square where Pierre lived.

"Wait here," she told me as she got out, but I ignored her.

She stood on the other side of the car, looking at me across the roof. "Why are you coming with me? I told you to wait here." She was wearing a light cotton blouse knotted beneath her breasts. She looked to me like a double-dipper ice-cream cone would to a ten-year old, but I kept my voice crisp.

"I'm doing my job."

She twisted her mouth into an angry knot of muscle, then jerked her head impatiently and stamped off toward Pierre's front door.

I locked the car, checking all around as I did so. There were no loiterers and no strange faces at any windows. Coming back to Pierre's house was not the smartest move we could have made, but this was Amy's research project, not a military operation.

There was nobody visible through the archway where I had half-hidden the day before, and I joined Amy at the door as she tugged on the old bell pull.

We heard it jangle deep in the house, but nobody answered. I flashed another look around the square—nobody there. "Is he usually in this time of day?" I asked.

"Always," she said. "He gets up at six and writes until noon. It's his routine. It never varies."

"Stand behind me." I pulled out my handkerchief and held it in my left hand. With my right I drew my pistol, keeping it out of sight from the square, flat in front of my body as I faced the door. Carefully I tried the door handle with my left, making sure not to wipe it as I did so. It opened, and I stepped in.

"Stay quiet and behind me," I whispered. She didn't make a sound, but followed as I took the three steps to the door of Pierre's study. It was closed, and I pushed it with the knuckles of my left hand. It swung inward, disclosing the cluttered desk, the books, the hard, empty chair, and finally, on the floor, a rusty stain that thickened and reddened as the door swung farther until it revealed Pierre's body, in the center of that ugly bloodstain that spread out a yard each way from the gash at his throat.

I didn't let her look. "Stay there," I said, not looking around. I held up my left hand to keep her from entering the room, but she had walked into it, allowing it to touch her breast. She gasped indignantly and slapped the hand away. "Watch it," she snapped. "Who do you think you are?"

I turned to her. "Pierre is dead. Don't move. Don't touch anything. We have to call Labrosse."

She gasped again, then craned around me, trying to see the body. "There's nothing you can do for him. We need the gendarmes. I'm just going to make sure there's nobody here."

I crouched and stepped into the doorway, my head at table height. There was nobody else there, and I could see that the bloodstain had spread out over the rug so wide that walking in the room would destroy evidence. I backed out and turned around, taking one look at Amy's white face and grabbing her by the elbow before she could collapse.

She let me grip her arm for about thirty seconds before regaining her composure and gently moving my hand away. At the outer door I stepped in front of her, holding the Walther under the flap of my jacket, glancing around the square. There was nobody out there, even on the rooftops. I hooked my head at Amy, and she followed me out.

I pulled the door closed, using my handkerchief again. "Okay. We need a phone, pronto."

"There's a hotel in the next square. It'll be quicker than trying to get some private phone," she said. Her calmness surprised me. She hadn't seen Pierre's body, but she knew what had happened to him. But she didn't collapse. Nor did she falter over the next ten minutes, through the use of the telephone and the wait while Labrosse and his men came screaming up the road from town, sirens hee-hawing loud enough to bring everyone in the old town into the square.

Labrosse took a moment to get the details from us, then left us with one of his men while he checked things out for himself. He was back out within five minutes, and he asked me to join him inside.

A gendarme in white gloves was standing outside Pierre's office. He pushed the door open for us, and Labrosse stuck his hands in his pockets and stood in the doorway, looking down at the body.

"What do you think?" he asked me.

I made the best inspection I could from that distance. The hands were bloody where Pierre had struggled to stop the bleeding, and his hair was ruffled. That looked interesting, and I said, "I'm a soldier, not a cop. But from the look of his hair I'd say someone snuck up behind him, grabbed him by the hair to force his head back, and cut his throat."

"One wonders why," Labrosse said dryly. "And one wonders why there are many little cuts, six, seven." He extended his finger and counted. "I see eight little cuts, in the neck, under the chin."

"You think he was tortured?"

He nodded. "I think the man with the knife talked to our friend for a while and then killed him."

"This has to be about Amy," I said. "I was beginning to think that he had told Orsini she was coming to town. This proves I was wrong."

"Perhaps. But I do not think he could take much pain, this man. If there was anything they wanted to know this morning, they know it now." He turned and listened to a new arrival, a man in plain clothes carrying a camera. He nodded, and the man began to photograph the scene. As the photographer crouched and clicked, Labrosse said, "You see his hands? They are not cut."

"That means there were two of them," I thought out loud. "One to use the knife, one to keep his hands out of the way."

"From the condition of the blood I would say this was done . . . per'aps one hour ago," Labrosse said. "Where were you at eight-thirty?"

"As you see, I only have one pair of hands, Captain, but Amy and I were out at La Fongeline."

"And you are moving out of that trap?" He didn't need to spell out for me that Pierre would have told them where Amy was staying. I knew they would have found out by this time, anyway.

"I've advised Amy to move. It would take a dozen men to keep her safe up that laneway." I looked him in the eye, soldier to soldier. "I wouldn't want to cause you any unnecessary work."

"The death of a tourist, perhaps two tourists, causes me much trouble," he said with a slight grin. "Where do you move to?"

"I'm not sure. Somewhere I have a better chance of doing my job."

"I have a suggestion," he said. His English had come all the way back, I noticed. His accent was still as strong, but he was getting around in the language better than most English-born speakers.

"Let me guess. You want her to go home." It should have been any cop's first choice.

"I do not think Ma'amselle Roger will leave," he said. "No. I was thinking per'aps you could move into my house. It is large; I live alone."

"It's up to Amy. Thank you for the offer, Captain. I'll tell her." So the good captain fancied his chances with my charge! Good. It lightened my load enormously. No doubt

Amy could take care of herself in the relationships department. A woman as attractive as she had slapped her share of roving hands.

"Come," he said abruptly. He led the way back out. Another car had arrived with two more men in it. He went to them first and gave them a crisp set of commands. They nodded respectfully and separated, going to the front doors of the houses on each side of Pierre's. A canvass. Good. Solid police work that might just give Labrosse a description of Pierre's last callers.

I'd left Amy sitting in the police car, and I went over and bent to speak to her through the window.

She looked up at me as if she had just woken up. "What did you say?"

"The captain has a place for us to stay. That's if you still want to stay now." I figured she wouldn't. Murder is nature's way of saying "listen up." And she had been close to Pierre.

She surprised me. "I think Pierre would want me to stay, to finish my work. We talked about it so much. He was proud that I was going to do it. His father was in a German prison camp. He hated them. He wanted me to celebrate the courage of the French people."

"I don't advise it. But it's your call."

"I will finish it and dedicate it to his memory." There. She had a reason, if she had needed one. This was one tough woman.

"So, okay, the captain says we can stay with him."

That thought didn't please her a lot. But she was practical now, concentrating on her work again. That much was good.

"If we don't, what do you suggest?"

"We'd have to look for a succession of places. We

couldn't stay anywhere longer than it would take to trace us. This way you've got double the protection and a permanent address."

"It looks as if I've won a heart," she said coolly. "Where is he?"

"Talking to his men. He'd like to know your answer." I opened the door, and she got out.

"This is humiliating," she said quietly. "I won't do it."

"Your choice, but we have to leave La Fongeline."

"You told me that," she said. "I am not moving in with some cop, that's all."

In the end she fielded the whole thing very well. Speaking in French too fast for me to follow in detail, she thanked him and refused, but there was a warmth in her voice that took any sting out of her words. Labrosse gave her a taut smile in return and a quick response, also in French I couldn't follow, and turned away.

We went back to our own car, and I opened the door for her. It was already hot in the square, the glorious high-sunned summer of the wine country, trapped by the old stone walls, and the interior of the car was like an oven. Amy didn't even notice. She was coming out of her numbness and beginning to understand what had happened to Pierre. Her eyes darted everywhere, and her fingers fidgeted, but she did not weep.

I started the motor and asked, "Where does Madame Boulanger live?"

"In the Place de Montfort, opposite Le Siècle," she said. And then, finally, she broke down and began to sob.

I glanced at her, unsure what to do. She had proved by her coolness up to that point that she didn't want me to make "there, there, poor thing" noises. But she was not ready to meet anybody. In the end I compromised.

There's a small lookout point next to an old church on a side street. I drove out on to it and got out of the car, dropping my handkerchief next to her on the seat without a word. Then I walked back to the entrance to the area and stood there, watching the road behind us for a few minutes until I saw Amy get out of the car and walk to the wall that overlooked the river and the new town below.

She turned as I rejoined her and gave me a watery smile, the first unstudied expression she'd worn since we'd found Pierre's body. "Thank you," she said, and tucked my handkerchief back into the breast pocket of my light jacket.

"You're welcome," I said, keeping it light. "Shall we get back where we Boulange?"

She snorted at my poor pun, and I drove us down to the village square. We found a parking spot under a plane tree, and she led me to a doorway in the solid wall of stores and apartments that made up one side of the square. There were four doorbells on the wall, and she rang the topmost one, then backed out into the street.

High above us a woman's voice asked, "Who's there?" in French. Amy replied, and there was a torrent of French and a tinkle on the sidewalk in front of us. Amy picked up the key and let us in for the four-story climb.

Madame Boulanger was waiting at her door, a frail-looking seventy-year-old. She and Amy greeted one another, but without kisses. They were new acquaintances. Amy introduced me, and the old woman shook hands. *"Enchantée."*

"Moi aussi," I said, and the old lady laughed and commented in rapid French. Amy translated, grinning. "The gist of that is, don't give up your day job, you'll never make it as a translator."

"Je promisse," I said, and the old lady cackled again.

We went into her apartment, which was furnished like an early cinema verité movie set, and she put coffee on. Then she and Amy started talking.

Amy had brought a tape recorder with her, and it turned silently as she chattered away with our hostess. I was lost except for the occasional word, but one word I did understand. Amy referred to Le Loup. And that brought Madame to a standstill. Her right hand fluttered to the brooch at her throat, and her lips pursed in anger. *"Il a tué mon mari,"* she said.

I didn't have any trouble understanding that message. Orsini had killed her husband.

CHAPTER

7

THE OLD LADY began to weep, and Amy moved beside her on the couch to comfort her. There were tears in her own eyes. She was not just a historian on this one. Perhaps she had thought that she could dull the pain of Pierre's death by working on her project, looking at her own life from the perspective of the past. Instead, she had stumbled across other sorrows, and they had added to her own.

I felt sorry for both women. I've lost a lot of friends over the years, good buddies I'd lived with and fought alongside in the shabby side streets of Ulster or the cold and rain of the Falklands. I know how it feels when death tears a hole in your life. As a soldier you expect it. Your grief is tempered by the thought that it could just as easily have been you going home in a body bag. As a civilian you don't get even that much icy comfort.

The only tactful thing to do was leave them for a while, so I moved out into the kitchen and stood at the window, looking down at the activity in the square. A couple in a convertible had driven in, lovers, laughing together while their car radio blared French rock music, but apart from that, the pace of life was what it had been for the last two centuries, slow and calming. Standing there was like watching a pageant.

After a while the voices next door became audible again, and I went back in. They had composed themselves, and the old lady was speaking slowly, recounting her memories of the night her husband died, speaking with dignity, slowly enough that I could follow.

Her husband had been a Communist. She said it with some pride in his shrewdness. The French have a tradition of socialism that dates back to the Revolution, and for many of his generation Stalin had seemed like the obvious antidote to Hitler. Anyway, somebody informed the Germans, and they came looking for him. His wife had been able to get word to him in the vineyard, and he dropped his tools and disappeared, joining the Maquis. From time to time he managed to sneak back at night to see her. She had even conceived a child on one occasion, a man in his forties now who had never known his father.

He had come one night and told her that something special was about to happen. Sloppy security—but understandable in a civilian. Madame had been far along in her pregnancy by that time, something that had made the German gauleiter in town suspicous, she added, until she had made a practice of seeming to flirt with the baffled *patron* of the butcher's shop. Her husband had heard about the flirting from some new Maquis recruit and had been jealous, she remembered, until she explained, and it was then he had told her about the action he was going into.

The Germans had shot down a British bomber, and one of the crew was in the local military hospital with a couple of broken legs. A British undercover officer had been parachuted in to the Maquis. Boulanger himself did not know it, but she had found out after the war that the airman was not a regular RAF man. He was a radar scientist, what the Brits call a boffin. The object of the exercise was to kill him before the Germans realized what he knew and went to work on him. In peacetime that thought is chilling, but in fact it was humane. An organization that produced people like Heinrich Himmler would have had no compunction about twisting his broken legs until he'd told them everything he knew. Then they would have shot him themselves, using the excuse that he was a spy.

On that August night, the young Boulanger had gone on the raid along with a score of other men, armed with the little Mickey Mouse Sten guns the British provided. The Sten cost about five bucks apiece to stamp out. It was inaccurate and unreliable, but it had the virtue of being able to use captured German ammunition.

The Germans were expecting Boulanger's group. Only two of the attackers survived. One was the British officer, who was taken to a concentration camp, where he eventually was shot. The other was Orsini.

At this point the old woman paused in her narrative, back in her stride now, telling the story the way she had obviously told it before. She refilled our coffee cups and waited for the question, which I put, in my own halting French: In what way had Orsini been responsible for her husband's death?

It was obvious, she explained. He had been the last recruit of the band of Resistance men her husband belonged to. Obviously, sadly, he had been a German plant. She shrugged. After all, had he not been the only survivor? All the locals and the British officer had been shot by the Germans.

Still in French, I persisted. Orsini had gone on to kill other Germans. Hostages had been shot because of his activities.

Madame shook her head, angry now. "The Germans said their men had been killed. No Frenchman had seen these dead Germans. It was an excuse for wiping out the prominent citizens of certain towns. The Germans had shot mayors and priests and other men. They had done it because they were Germans, for no other reason. *Sales Boches!* They needed no reason."

It didn't sound like the kind of soldiering I'd been taught to do. It wasn't even classic Clausewitz, but Madame had been here, on the ground, and my father hadn't even met my mother at that point, so what did I know? I nodded and fell silent. It still didn't ring true to me. The French had been hard on their collaborators after the war, when there were no Germans around to protect them. They had shaved the heads of any girls who had gone out with a German. They had shot or hanged known male collaborators. Surely some Maquisard would have taken revenge on Orsini after the war, before he grew big enough to have his own organization. I kept the thought to myself while Amy went back to work.

She was interested in the story, but she had her own priorities, and she took over again. First she followed up on the hospital affair until all the details were on her tape and all the proper sympathies expressed. Then she steered Madame down the paths she wanted to explore, digging out names and places and details until the old woman began to flag.

As soon as she saw the weariness begin, Amy brought the interview to a close. She invited Madame to join us for lunch, and when the old lady smilingly refused, telling us how difficult it was for her to negotiate the stairs to the street, Amy first offered to shop for food and cook lunch for her, then, when that failed, gracefully made her a present of some cash.

We left her beaming at the door and headed down to the street. "How does she manage if she can't come downstairs?" I wondered, and Amy explained that her daughter-in-law did the shopping for her.

"What a life. Sitting up there with sad memories, waiting for the curé to bring communion once a week," I said.

"She's part of the life of the town," Amy said. "She lives at the window."

We got to the car and looked back up at the building. Madame was indeed back at her window, looking down at the comings and goings in the square. "Isn't she better off here than in some seniors' residence, watching soap operas while the TV picture rolls because nobody in charge can bother to fix it?" Amy said. She waved up to the old woman, who waved back and blew her a kiss.

It was noon, and the stores around the square were closing for the lunch hour. The restaurants on the east side were beginning to fill, but we found a table under the awning at a place a couple of doors up from Le Siècle.

"I ate here once last year. The food is nowhere near as good as it is at Le Siècle," Amy said.

"It's harder to hit a moving target," I told her. "If you get into routines, like always eating at the same restaurant, it won't take people long to ambush you."

She shrugged. "I'm not hungry, anyway. I came here for your sake."

"Then this place is fine for me. But you should have something. You must eat. Believe me."

She looked at me soberly but didn't argue, and I ordered

a glass of wine and an omelet for both of us and asked her, "What're you planning to do this afternoon?"

She twirled her wineglass in her fingers. "I want to talk to Jacques Beaubien. He's the next one on my list. But he has to be close to eighty. He probably rests during the heat of the day."

"You should do the same thing. How about we find a hotel and check in right away? Then you can get a couple of hours' sleep."

She shook her head, and before I could speak again, I saw a car slam to a stop on the street opposite our table.

I put down my wineglass and slid my right hand under my coat, where I could reach my gun. I braced my legs under me, ready to stand and bat Amy down on the deck and return fire if I had to.

The door opened, and a man got out, tall and elderly, distinguished looking. I didn't relax completely. Orsini might have brought in the guy for a custom killing, and it was likely that I, not Amy, was to be the target. They would hit me and whisk her away before the echo of her screams had stopped bouncing off the walls of the square. "Do you know this guy?" I asked her.

She turned anxiously and then stood up and almost ran to him, speaking to him in rapid French. I saw that she was weeping again and caught the name: "M'sieur Armand." He was well dressed, in his seventies. I stood and waited as Amy kissed him on both cheeks and held both his hands in hers. He replied gravely, but too fast for my French to keep up. Then Amy turned to me.

"May I present Mr. Locke. John, this is M'sieur Armand, Pierre's father."

He held out his hand. It was soft but strong. "*Enchanté*, M'sieur Locke."

"How do you do, sir. May I offer my sincere condolences on your loss."

He nodded without speaking, and Amy asked him something in French, but he said, "Should we not speak English, Amy, or does M'sieur Locke also speak French?"

"Very poorly, I'm ashamed to say."

"In that case . . ." His English was good, accented charmingly, like Maurice Chevalier but grammatical. "To answer your question, yes, Hélène is with me. She is in the car."

"Can she join us?" Amy was looking around, and Armand pointed across the road to his car, a classic Bentley.

"Please continue your lunch. I will bring her over."

He nodded again and walked away, up to the car. We stood and watched him, as he opened the back door. A chic blond woman got out. She was about thirty, slim in that lissome way that shouts "money!" She was wearing one of those simple-looking linen suits you can pick up in Paris for a couple of thousand dollars, and a straw boater, what the French call a Maurice.

She turned, and even from thirty yards away I could see she was a knockout, her face a classic oval, her hair pertly short in a way that almost mocked her beauty.

"Daughter or wife?" I asked Amy without turning my head.

Amy's voice had the first hint of lightness I'd heard since the discovery of the murder. "Daughter, but don't waste your charm," she said with a touch of her old nastiness. "She'll chew you up."

Frenchmen are more blasé about beautiful women than the rest of us. They spend their lives among them. Every woman in the country makes the utmost of her appearance, in simple ways that only rich women in North America ever manage to duplicate, but Hélène turned every head on the street. She came toward us, her face unmoving. It could have been sorrow at her brother's death or, given Amy's caution, her normal hauteur.

She and Amy exchanged ritual kisses, bussing the air close to both sides of one another's cheeks, and Amy said something sympathetic in French. Hélène responded, and Amy introduced me.

Hélène nodded at me, appraising me. "Mister Locke."

"Ma'amselle." I inclined my head a couple of inches. "May I say how sorry I am at what has happened."

"Thank you." She sat down at our table, and her father pulled a chair over from the next table and sat next to her. Amy and I sat, and the waiter bustled over, coming to the table opposite Hélène, where he could fill his eyes with her.

"Deux cafés," Armand said, and the waiter almost ran back to the counter.

I waited for Amy to do the talking, enjoying my view of the fair Hélène. Up close she was even more striking. Her face looked like something off a gold coin. It was as close to perfection as I've ever seen, and I guess I've sized up every woman I've met since puberty.

"When did you hear?" Amy asked.

"A Captain Labrosse of the Gendarmerie called about an hour ago," Armand said softly. "We have just come from the morgue."

The memory knocked Hélène's English out from under her. I made out "Mon dieu!" but lost track of her next few sentences.

Armand headed her back into English with his question for Amy.

"What is happening?" Armand asked softly, speaking

almost to himself. "My God. A scholar, working at his books. No robbery, no reason."

Amy didn't answer; she just shook her head, tears forming in the corners of her eyes.

Armand patted her hand. He was very much in control of himself, and so was Hélène. They must have figured it was lower-class to let your grief hang out. "Do the gendarmes say anything?"

"The captain wonders if there is a connection with what happened yesterday," I volunteered. "In case you didn't hear, Amy was attacked, and Pierre came to her assistance." It wasn't as true as it sounded, but they deserved a little compensation for the loss of son and brother.

Armand looked at me in surprise, but Hélène spoke before he could. "You are police, m'sieur?" Her voice had a casual arrogance to it, an assumption that I was some kind of lackey. Even had I been Amy's fiancé rather than her bodyguard, she would have sounded the same. As my sister the shrink would have put it, women like her divide the world into "me" and "not me." The "not me" segment doesn't matter a damn."

"No. I work for Miss Roger's uncle."

"In what capacity?"

"On assignment to assist Amy during her visit."

"John is a bodyguard," Amy said impatiently. "Eric insisted. He asked John to come with me in case something happened." Hélène still did not look impressed, so she added, "John was in the British army."

"But you are American," Armand said gently.

"Canadian." If he hadn't been burdened with his bereavement, he might have been amused to hear my reasons for joining the British army. Canadian servicemen wear green, even our navy, and they spend most of their time

in boring places like northern Saskatchewan. I'd wanted
action, which the Brits provided for me. But Armand was
in pain, so I didn't make any jokes. I sat and waited, hoping
to learn something that might give a hint as to why his son
had died.

He spoke to Amy. "Is there any connection, do you
think?"

Amy couldn't answer. She wept openly.

Hélène got to her feet and took Amy's arm. "*Viens-toi,*"
she said, and led her away. I stood up and watched them
go, certain that Hélène was taking her somewhere private
to compose herself, but not sure where. I relaxed when I
saw Hélène open the back door of the car but wave the
chauffeur away. They were going to sit there awhile. In
Canada they would have headed for the ladies' room. In
Provence that was impossible. In a bistro like this the john
was probably unisex and consisted of a spartan booth with
an intimidating hole in the floor. Not the kind of powder
room where tears might be dried.

I sat down again and looked at Armand. "This is a
harrowing morning for you, M'sieur Armand. Would you
like a cognac?"

"Yes, thank you. Now my daughter is gone." He
shrugged. "The doctors."

I raised my hand, and the waiter came out. "*Un cognac
pour m'sieur, s'il vous plaît.*" I can order drinks in a lot
of languages.

He whisked back to the bar and returned with the
tiny snifter. Armand gulped it, making a face. I used his
grimace to change the subject. "You deal in wine, Amy
told me."

"One does not need to be a dealer to appreciate quality,"

he said. He set down the glass and looked at me steadily. "What is happening here, Mr. Locke?"

"I don't know, sir." I sipped my wine. "I was hired because Amy told her uncle she had trouble last year from a hood called Orsini. Yesterday, just after we arrived, two men attempted to abduct her outside Pierre's house in the Haute-Ville."

"And what happened to these men?"

"They were arrested." I kept it simple.

"The gendarmes were there when it happened?"

"No. Pierre called them after the event."

"You prevented this abduction?"

The gesture must be contagious. I never shrug at home, but I did now. "It's why I'm along on the trip."

"And Pierre, he assisted you?" There was an eagerness in his voice. His son was dead; he would never have another chance to be proud of him. Had he been brave?

I shaded the truth. "Yes."

He looked almost happy. "Then it was revenge, his death."

"That makes the most sense."

The waiter was hovering, and Armand picked up his cognac glass and held it out. The man nodded and was about to return to the bar, but Armand stopped him with a quick sentence. The waiter nodded and bustled away, returning with two glasses, one for each of us.

Armand sipped his and rolled it in his mouth, then nodded to the waiter. "You will find this one better," he said.

I did. It was liquid sunshine, languid on the tongue. "That's glorious. What is it?"

Armand smiled. "I asked him for *une fine plus fine*—something better." He sipped his own, savoring it as he was savoring the thought of his son's fighting a couple of heavies to protect Amy. At last he went on. "Pierre was not young, not a fighting man, but perhaps capable of fight. That must have been why this happened."

It was time to do a little fishing. "I think he was also helping Amy with her new project. This time it is very different."

He cocked his head. "Not the Romans?"

"No. She is writing a book on the Resistance in this region."

"One wonders who would be offended by such a book." He rolled his cognac glass idly between his hands, looking down into it. He was a strong-looking man, despite his age, but the gesture made him frail.

"There is a tie to this man Orsini," I said. "The old woman Amy spoke to this morning mentioned his name. She said he was a traitor to the Resistance. She also said that he was known as Le Loup."

He looked up bleakly. "You were a soldier, Mr. Locke. Have you ever seen war?"

"Only little ones. The Falklands, Ulster."

He nodded, a small rocking motion of head and shoulders together. "They are never over," he said softly. "When the last survivor dies, after many years, even then, they do not end."

"You were in the war, M'sieur Armand?"

"I was in Germany, a prisoner, captured in 1940 before I had a chance to fight. My government threw up its hands."

"It saved the lives of many Frenchmen." The way I've heard it, there was not a whole lot of heroism in France in 1940. The railway stations of Paris had been flooded with officers in civilian clothes heading for the unoccupied zone when they should have been at the front with their men. The only safe thing to praise the French for was their prudence.

"We should have fought to the last man," Armand said bitterly. "We should never have collaborated in our own rape."

An old man's shame is not something to share. My glass was almost empty, but I pretended to sip. And then help arrived. Labrosse strode across the square and halted the traffic with one hand, coming directly to our table. I stood up. "Captain Labrosse, M'sieur Armand, the father of Pierre."

Labrosse saluted crisply and spoke in French. Armand answered and Labrosse turned to me. "Where is Miss Roger?"

"She is in that auto with M'sieur Armand's daughter."

"I will talk to her there. Please come with me." He bowed his head formally to Armand and led the way to the car.

The Armands had a chauffeur, I discovered, a compact guy with a Mediterranean swarthiness. He was in his forties, wearing black pants, a white shirt with bow tie, and a cap. He was wiping down the hood of the car with a rag.

Amy and Hélène were in the backseat. Hélène had her arm around Amy's shoulder. Labrosse tapped on the window on Hélène's side and, when she wound down the window, excused himself in rapid French. She got out, and he got in, gesturing to me to sit in the front.

"It seems this was a robbery," Labrosse said without preamble. "M'sieur Armand was a careful man. He had money in the house. It is gone."

"May I ask how you learned this, Captain?" I asked.

"I think it was a robbery," he said again, as if I were a

backward boy. "His cleaning woman says the money was kept in a book on his desk. It is gone."

"Do you get much of this?" I asked. Amy was composed again, but she didn't look likely to say very much.

"Theft? *D'accord*," Labrosse said. "The cutting of throats, no."

"Did you find the murder weapon?"

"Why would you ask that, m'sieur?" Labrosse wanted to know.

"Because it could mean that Pierre recognized the man who robbed him and was killed with whatever was at hand."

"We found no weapon," he said, and then added inconsequentially, "The cut was made by a right-handed man."

"So we're looking for a right-handed man with a knife. In wine country, where most of the men work in the vineyards, that has to be most of the male population."

Labrosse rubbed his chin, making a faint rasping sound. "Tell me, Miss Roger. About what did you talk to Madame Boulanger today?"

"The Resistance. Her husband was a member. He was killed in 1944. Why do you ask, is this important?"

He didn't reply at once. Without asking if she objected, he took out his cigarettes and lit up, flicking the dead match casually out the window. "And what else did she say?"

"Why don't you ask her yourself?" Amy was getting acerbic, her grief all burned away in righteous anger. Good; she was easier to handle mad than sad.

"She told you perhaps that the man Orsini was known as Le Loup?" He dropped the question in casually. Apparently Amy's scoop was not as exclusive as she'd imagined.

"Among other things," Amy said tensely. I glanced at her as she spoke. Her hand had come up to her throat. She was worried. Was it professional concern about her sources or anxiety about her own safety?

"And these other things, did any of them concern people now living?" He was patient, the way he would have been patient in a cell in Algeria during the civil war, waiting for his man to beat a confession out of some terrorist. You get the same kind of calm at the eye of a cyclone.

"Only her son." Amy was back in stride now, as high-handed as ever. "Why do you ask?"

He changed the subject. "Tell me, ma'amselle. Do you think that Armand was killed for a handful of francs?"

She was baffled and turned to me. It was time to act like a gentleman. "I think perhaps someone who discovered the body may have known where he kept his money and taken it."

"Do you, M'sieur Locke?" His voice was icy. "May I remind you that it was you who discovered the body."

"I was the one who reported finding the body," I corrected him. "Do you know who else visited him this morning?"

He blew smoke. "You are an expert on theft, perhaps?"

"I know something about death, Captain. That death was not in keeping with a theft." I got bold and made the suggestion that had occurred to me when he mentioned theft. "I do not wish to question the honesty of his housekeeper, if he has one. But perhaps she took the money, although I don't think a woman cut his throat."

"Very good," he said dryly. "And finding this money will raise Armand from the dead?"

"Nothing will do that, Captain."

"Now you begin to understand," he said. "All we can

do is to look for the man who killed him and prevent such an incident from happening again. To a policeman, the cure is simple. Miss Roger talks to someone, they die. I say to you, Miss Roger, that you must stop talking to people. Then they will stop dying."

"But I came here to work on my book," Amy spluttered.

"And this book is more important than the lives of Frenchmen?" Labrosse showed his disgust by snuffing out his cigarette between finger and thumb and tossing it away.

Amy was controlled again now. "Of course not. No book is worth lives, Captain. But how can you be sure this is cause and effect?"

"I cannot be sure that a man who has consumed a liter of cognac will kill people as he drives home," Labrosse said. "I merely remove him from the road if I see him near a car."

"Are you telling me I've got to leave?" Amy asked.

"A professor such as yourself knows better than that," he said. "I am telling you that I suspect you of complicity in the murder of Pierre Armand. I am not going to arrest you, but if someone you spoke to were even to slip on the street and scratch his knee, I will arrest you and charge you with the murder."

Anger blazed in her eyes. "You have no right. John, tell him he has no right." She almost yelled it.

I shook my head. "This is the captain's town, Amy. He makes the rules."

"Damn you," she said. "Damn all men." She got out of the car, slamming the door. Labrosse sat calmly, looking me right in the eye. Deliberately, he got out his cigarettes and lit up again.

"She isn't going to quit, Captain," I said.

He nodded, squinching up one eye against the smoke

from his Gauloise. "I know that," he said. "But do you know why she is so determined to continue?"

"She told me it's important to her position at the university." I shrugged. "It seems odd to me. Her field was the Roman occupation of Provence. Now she's skipping two thousand years to talk about the German occupation. I wonder why."

"I also wonder why," he said. "Many books have been written about the Resistance. None of them has been important enough to risk a life for. Then we have this girl insisting suddenly on writing, and at the same time, we have a murder. As a policeman, I wonder why."

"I appreciate the need-to-know rule, Captain," I said carefully. "But it sounds as if you have information you have not conveyed to me. For instance, you haven't mentioned Orsini in all this. He's the one with the grudge against Amy. It seems logical to me that he's the guy who did this killing. Or had it done for him."

He drew on his cigarette, narrowing his eyes the way smokers do, studying me hard. At last he said, "I think you are a soldier, M'sieur Locke, so I will tell you." I didn't change my expression, and he went on slowly. "I have investigated the event last year." He paused and waved vaguely. "The incident at the restaurant which was the commencement of all this."

"The night she clobbered Orsini?"

He nodded. "Yes. One heard that Miss Roger was having dinner when Orsini first spoke to her, then molested her. Then, one hears, she hit him with the wine bottle."

"And this didn't happen?"

"No." He let the word hang there alone, filling the car like the smoke from his cigarette.

"And what were the facts?"

Now he became formal, as he might have been with a witness. "You and Miss Roger are close?"

"I work for her, that's all."

"Then perhaps you will not be too desolated to hear that she spent the night with him," he said.

I guess my jaw dropped. He reacted with a tight smile. "Yes, I was surprised also."

"But the story didn't end there. Apparently one of the film people was beaten because he laughed in the restaurant. And Constance at La Fongeline called out all her old Resistance buddies and stood guard. You mean that's all lies as well?"

"The film man was beaten," he said. "But the reason was quite different. When Orsini and Miss Roger left the restaurant, he took Orsini's woman to his room. Poor fool must have thought it was love; he refused to pay, and one of Orsini's men punished him."

I whistled in surprise. "That puts a very different complexion on things. But what about the old Resistance people at Constance's farm? What about Amy leaving the next morning to return to Canada?"

He shrugged again, his face expressionless. "One thinks perhaps Constance is a good friend to Miss Roger. This story was prepared as an alibi."

"Why in hell would she need an alibi? She can sleep with any man she chooses to," I said, but the answer had already occurred to me. The truth had to be kept from Wainwright. He was obviously Amy's lover, protector, whatever, in Canada. It looked as if Janet Frobisher's thoughts had been on the right track.

"She has no husband?" he asked carefully. "No one who would find such news unpleasant?"

I considered my answer carefully. Labrosse was leveling with me; I owed him the same courtesy. "I was hired by an older man. He says he is Miss Roger's uncle."

Labrosse lowered the corners of his mouth. *"Peut-être."* Perhaps.

I sucked my teeth thoughtfully. "This is very interesting, Captain, but it doesn't explain why those two guys tried to abduct Amy yesterday or why somebody cut that man's throat this morning. What's going on?"

He had only half-smoked his cigarette, but he took it out of his mouth and tossed it out the window angrily. "That is what I need to know," he said.

"May I ask why you haven't questioned Amy about this?"

"Sometimes in an investigation it is better to observe, to act slowly."

"What do you expect to learn from the observation?"

He shrugged again, slowly, almost a caricature of the gesture. "If I talk to her at once, I may perhaps learn something of what has happened before. But I already know much of that. I do not believe she knows why her friend Armand was murdered. That is the only event that concerns me."

"How about the two men I stopped yesterday? What did they tell you?"

"They were sent by a man in Marseilles. Alas, they do not know his name. They were sent to bring Miss Roger to Marseilles, to this man."

"Did they give you a description at least?"

"It would fit most of the men in Marseilles between the ages of thirty and sixty years." Labrosse opened the door of the car and half-turned to get out. "And so the work continues. In the meantime, I wish that Miss Roger does not speak to anyone else. Can you convince her of the need for this?"

"I'll sure as hell try, Captain. Thank you for your confidences." I turned away, wondering why Amy had lied about Orsini and what the fact meant to me.

CHAPTER

8

THE OTHERS were standing up, preparing to go. "We're going to stay with M'sieur Armand and Hélène," Amy told me.

"Fine," I said. "Thank you, m'sieur."

He nodded, and Hélène told Amy, "You know where we are. We have things to attend to. We will see you at the house later."

"You're very kind." Amy was on the brink of tears, but Hélène brushed off the thanks impatiently. "You should have called us."

They went back to their car, and I led Amy over to ours. I glanced up at Madame Boulanger's window. She was at her post.

Constance's old car was missing when we went back to La Fongeline, so Amy wrote her a quick note explaining what had happened. It covered two pages, so it must have gone into a fair amount of detail, but it was her concern. I left the book Constance had lent me on the bed and put the bags into the car, looking over my shoulder the whole time. I didn't say a lot to Amy. I wanted to know all about Orsini and try to get to the bottom of what was happening, but that would have to wait. For now, it seemed, nobody was after her.

The Armands were staying in a château located in one of their vineyards. It was a second residence, Amy told me briefly. They lived in Paris most of the time, where the senior Armand had his offices, dealing with wines from all of the regions of France. But he had started out here, in his ancestral home, and still kept an apartment in the château, which was also occupied by the factor of the estate.

Set among vineyards, it was a handsome late-nineteenth-century brick building with a half acre of lawn and old oak trees around it. The resident family lived in an apartment on the ground floor, leaving the major rooms free for the owners, Amy had told me. They had made themselves at home, it seemed. There was a clutter of young children playing around the house, swinging on a rope hanging from an oak limb, laughing and calling out like kids anywhere.

Madame came to the door when Amy knocked and insisted on helping us in with the bags. She was a round-faced, happy woman, as close to plain as any Frenchwoman ever gets but pert and cheerful.

She was not sure of our domestic setup, and so she put all the bags in the bigger spare bedroom. Amy was subdued and didn't argue, but we didn't do any unpacking. Instead, we accepted her invitation to coffee on the terrace and went down to sit and and watch the children playing and wait for the Armands to arrive.

Forcing herself to make conversation, Amy asked, "What do you think of Hélène?"

"Sensational," I said. "I've worked for movie stars that can't hold a candle to her." I was watching Amy, trying to read her emotions. She had seen more violence in the last twenty-four hours than had happened in her whole life, and here she was chatting like a cocktail-party guest. Either she had no heart, or she was hanging on to her sanity by her fingertips.

"Don't lose your heart over Hélène." She said it lightly, but it came out almost bitchy.

I grinned agreeably. "I leave my heart at home when I'm working." My glands travel with me, but I didn't tell her that.

"Very professional," she said. And then the Bentley rolled in, and we got up to meet our hosts.

Hélène soon set the domestic arrangements straight. Amy stayed along the hall from her on the second floor. I was moved up to the third. I said nothing, but the arrangement didn't please me. I hadn't seen any security arrangements around the house. There was a dog, but it was a children's pet, small and silent. A professional could get into the house and murder Amy, or even abduct her, without anybody's knowing. I would have to make changes.

We were invited to share a late lunch with the Armands. Amy and I sat and sipped wine while the other two picked at their food. Nobody said much, and afterward Armand went to his room. The women sat and talked, soon lapsing into French, a clear signal that I wasn't welcome.

I took the hint and excused myself and went outside to check the lay of the land.

It was a typical Provençal summer day, sunny, the temperature in the high eighties. The heat had slowed down even the kids, and they were sitting in the shade of a tree having a serious-seeming conversation. I walked all around the house. The garage was at the back, and I found the chauffeur washing the car, unnecessarily, moving slowly, filling time. He smiled when I spoke to him but made no attempt to answer, so I didn't push it but walked on. The only useful thing I noticed was that the roof of the garage, formerly the stables by the look of it, reached to the second floor of the main house, giving access to a window. I rechecked the map of the interior in my mind and saw that the window must be in Amy's room.

She and Hélène were still talking when I returned. They looked up when I came in. Hélène spoke first. "Yes?"

Regal women leave me cold. I was once dumb enough to fall for the daughter of an earl, the sister of a fellow officer in the Guards. It ended when she broke her claws trying to make me feel small. "Excuse me," I said, and spoke to Amy. "Your room has a roof outside, right?"

"I think so." Canadian women don't have the knack of superiority. They're still busy trying to prove they're equal.

"I don't like it. Any guy who isn't in a wheelchair could be over that roof and into your room like a shot."

Hélène spoke first; I would have bet on that. "My friend is in the guest room," she said.

I ignored her. "If you're staying there, I'd suggest you leave the door unlocked, and I'll sleep in the corridor."

Hélène was about to speak, but Amy beat her to it. "You think someone will follow us here?"

"If they're after you, yes. You're gift-wrapped and waiting if you sleep in that bedroom."

Hélène picked up the bell she'd used to call Madame during lunch and spoke to Amy in French. I made out the word *lit*, bed.

"No," I said firmly. "Thank you, anyway. Don't tell Madame. She doesn't need to know, and I don't want a bed."

Hélène stretched her elegant cheeks in a mocking smile. "You are hoping to use someone else's?"

I looked at her and sighed. She flushed; I'd trumped her ace.

Amy said. "You think someone would climb over the roof to reach me?"

"Somebody is serious enough to have killed Pierre. Until the gendarmes catch whoever it is, you're in danger."

Hélène said, "Not while you stay here, Amy. Papa will have men patrol the grounds at night."

"I can't just hide like this," Amy burst out. "I came here to do a job."

I answered that one. "It will wait a few days or weeks. You heard what the captain said. You can't go back to questioning people. If anything goes sour, he'll lock you up."

Amy stood up angrily. "I'm going to rest," she said. "I'll be in my room, Hélène, if you'll excuse me."

Hélène only nodded. I stood aside to let Amy pass, and then Hélène spoke. "Would you like a glass of wine?"

Nobody would attempt to go over the roof in daylight, I was off duty for an hour, so I nodded. "Thank you."

She poured us both a glass and handed mine to me.

I raised it to her. "A votre santé."

"Well done," she said mockingly. "And to your health."

It was time to get her support. Amy was still at risk, I was certain of it. If I was thrown out of the house for being unreasonable, it would mean sneaking about the grounds all day instead of staying close to Amy. I had to play nice. "I am very sad about your brother. I met him only once, but he was a good, gentle man."

"Gentle, yes." She sipped her wine and sat with her right elbow cradled in her left hand, looking into the glass. It was as formal as an art deco sculpture.

"Not good?" I made the question gentle.

"If good is the absence of positive evil, then yes, he was good."

"I seem to have disturbed something. I'm sorry." It wasn't

clear whether or not she was flirting. If she was, I figured it was only because she didn't have a good book with her.

"He was wasting his life with his silly writing." She was angry now, controlled but venting steam like an over-stressed boiler.

"I thought he was a scholar."

"So did he." She set down her wineglass. "He should have been working with Papa."

"But now you do that instead of Pierre." Amy had given me that much on the ride over. And she was probably excellent at business. She was cool and brisk, and very few men would have had the heart to haggle with her. Just one million-watt flash of her smile and they would cheerfully pay through their noses for the family's plonk.

"This is boring you," she said.

"On the contrary. I've been parachuted into the middle of a mystery. Anything I can learn is likely to help me."

"How?" A fair question, but she used it like an ax, swinging it with real weight.

"His death was no doubt connected with the fact that someone tried to abduct Amy yesterday. Find his killer and we find out what's happening."

"I'll tell you what's happening," she said suddenly. "Someone is declaring war."

"On whom?" Well done. An educated woman like Hélène would appreciate the "m."

She shrugged and picked up her wine again, not posing, just gripping it as if it were her only connection to sanity. She was angry, I saw, and frightened, but she was not grieving. A very cold fish. "Perhaps my father."

"You mean some business competitor? Surely they wouldn't get around to murder? Especially of Pierre. You say he wasn't connected to the business."

"He is, was"—she shook her head impatiently—"the most important person in my father's life. Since my mother died last year."

"It still doesn't make sense. If someone wanted to pressure your father, they would have threatened Pierre, they wouldn't have killed him. That throws away their advantage."

"Logically, yes." She sipped her wine and set the glass down. We might have been discussing a soccer game, for all the emotion she was showing. "But my father is weak. His heart. This will crush him. It could even kill him."

"And then who takes over? Are you a public company?"

"No. We are a family concern." She pointed at her left breast with her right index finger. The nail was a perfect filbert shape and a quarter inch longer than her fingertip. The breast was world-class. "When Papa goes, we becomes me."

"But where does Amy fit into this? Why was someone trying to drag her into a car with Marseilles plates?"

"Did nobody tell you?" She smiled again. My not trying to impress her was impressing her. I figured she planned to win my heart and then gleefully jump up and down on it in high heels.

"I was hired to protect her from a man called Orsini." I said. "But from what I heard today from Captain Labrosse, that's a crock."

"What did he tell you?" She snapped out the question.

"It's confidential."

"Then why did you suggest something?" She was sneering now. If the carrot of her smile wouldn't work, she'd try the stick.

"Because somebody is after her. Somebody who was angry enough at missing her to kill your brother for his part in her rescue. I thought perhaps you knew something that might help me do my job."

"The gendarmes will find these people." She sipped her wine and then rummaged in her purse for cigarettes. I made no attempt to light up for her. The rough-hewn caper was working.

"It may take them months. In the meantime, I think she's in danger. Have you any idea why?"

"No," she said. She blew out the match and dropped it in the ashtray. "But I know what you are speaking of. I was with Amy when she met Orsini."

"Were you?" I shook my head. "If I may make a personal comment, ma'amselle, I find it hard to believe that he would have approached Amy with you at the same table."

"Explain yourself," she snapped, but I could see she had got my drift. She wanted to hear the compliment in full, that was all.

"Amy is attractive; you are beautiful. Unless this man had some kind of hidden agenda, something to do with Amy's being North American, I fail to understand his action." There, lady, what do you say to that?

She milked it. "Are you paying me a compliment, Mr. Locke?" she asked almost coquettishly.

"Just imagine I'm giving evidence," I said. "The facts, ma'am, just the facts."

"He approached our table," she said. "When I did not reply to him and Amy did, he concentrated his attentions upon her."

"The girls all get beautiful at closing time." I grinned. "And then what? You said good night to Amy and left her drinking wine and talking about the good old days with Signor Orsini?"

"You do not find her beautiful?"

"I'm working for her, or for her uncle. I don't mix business and personal feelings." It sounded good even though it wasn't true. And there's a big chunk of business sense in getting close to the woman you're guarding. You can spend your nights outside her door with one ear open or inside her room, where you're at hand if anything occurs. I'm all business, really.

"I think you have spent too much time with the English," she said, smiling as shyly as Lady Di. "Your blood has become cold."

"It's as red as ever. I have a job to do, that's all." This was a lot more fun than sitting upstairs reading a book, waiting for Amy to come out of her room and make herself a target again.

"Does she know what this gendarme told you?" She nudged me back on track.

"Not yet. I plan to discuss it with her to see if she can explain who might be threatening her in all this."

"And how will you pass the time until you have an opportunity to talk to her?" The invitation floated across the table as tangible as a visiting card.

"I have to stay in the house, but I'm open to suggestions."

She stood up, crushing her cigarette on her plate, ignoring the ashtray. "Come with me," she said harshly.

She led the way upstairs, pausing at the top to turn and put her finger to her lips. I inclined my head and followed, walking softly, my excitement rising with every step.

She stopped at Amy's room, tapped at the door, and then opened it and slipped inside, pushing the door shut behind her. She was out a minute later and closed the door carefully, nodding her head along the corridor. I followed, and she opened the door of her own room and turned to beckon me.

I went in after her and closed the door, noticing that the wall was almost a foot thick. Even though Daddy was next door, he wouldn't hear anything unless we started yelling at one another.

The room was huge and sported a business-sized bed. She stood by it and turned to face me, smiling now. I wasn't sure if this was a spider-and-fly party. She had me in her web now. She could holler "Rape" and have me arrested if she wanted to. No French cop would believe I'd been invited in. I stood there, looking at her, frankly admiring her beauty but not moving in.

"You are frightened, perhaps?" she asked, smiling.

"Not frightened. It's just that I'm a little too old to believe in Santa Claus."

"Perhaps you will change your mind," she said, and came over to me. I stood while she slid her arms around my neck and kissed me, softly, a very practiced kiss. At that point my hormones took over from my conscience, and I responded, moving slowly, one arm around her waist, the other caressing the nape of her neck. She sighed and then gently stood away from me and undressed, slowly, teasingly, like someone opening an expensive present.

First she unbuttoned the jacket of her suit, dropping it casually behind her. Under it she had a cream satin blouse, which she unbuttoned carefully, from the top, then the cuffs, then wriggling if off her shoulders so it shucked like the skin of some white snake. She was wearing a brassiere with fine lace across the top of her breasts. I was ungentlemanly enough to notice that the opaque bottom half seemed to have some kind of bone in it to take the strain.

Now she reached around herself and unzipped her skirt, pushing it down over her hips so that it and her slip slid down with a faint swish of fine fabrics rubbing together.

She was wearing cream-colored flare-legged panties over an honest-to-god garter belt with white stockings, something you only ever see on the Benny Hill TV show. The effect was heart-stopping. Lord, she'd even left her high heels on.

I managed to avoid saying, "Wow," but only because I put my arms around her and kissed her again, concentrating first on the kiss and then on unsnapping the brassiere. It came away, and I bent my head and kissed her breasts, tugging at her nipples with my lips until she groaned and started unfastening my belt impatiently.

She was like the survivor of some disaster, reassuring herself that she was alive. I tried manfully to pace us, but she dragged me backward onto the bed, and we came together in a frenzy.

Afterward I expected her to pull away, disgusted with herself and therefore with me. It had all been too precipitate, grief for her dead brother, anger, I wasn't sure what, except that I don't ever think of myself as God's gift, especially to a woman as beautiful as this. But she didn't. She clung to me, not fiercely, as if she were afraid I'd get up and drop a couple of hundred francs on the mantelpiece, but as if we were longtime lovers with an architecture to our relationship. I kissed her again, and soon we made love a second time, more slowly, savoring one another, giving as well as taking.

After that she slept, and I lay wondering what had triggered the explosion. Had it really happened because I'd been cool? Or was she like so many beautiful women, so intimidating to men that they get far fewer advances than they should because guys just figure they wouldn't stand a chance, so why get their egos damaged? It was a mystery, but I didn't care if I ever solved it.

In the end I got up. She moaned in her sleep but did not wake up, so I got dressed and sat across the room from her, marveling at her looks. I'm not a scorekeeper. Making love to a woman doesn't diminish her in my eyes. She was just as beautiful as she had been an hour ago, but I couldn't help wondering what her reaction was going to be when she was vertical again.

As I sat there, I heard a car crunching over the gravel. I looked out through the jalousies and saw a big black Daimler pull up in front. It got me moving. I went over to the bed and woke her, speaking softly.

She stirred and then sat up, startled. "What is it?"

"A car just arrived. It looks like it could have an executive in it. That probably means someone will come and wake your father. I should go."

She was very French. *"D'accord,"* she said, and gave me a brisk kiss on the lips.

I winked at her and left, checking the corridor to make sure Papa wasn't prowling. He wasn't, so I went up to my bedroom and retrieved the book I'd brought with me from home, Bruce Catton's *Stillness at Appomattox*. Then I came back down to the second floor and sat on the top step with the open book on my knees. I'm a big fan of General Lee's, and now, all languid from my time with Hélène, I was prepared to sit there all afternoon if I had to, reliving his triumphs and final disappointment. But I didn't get the chance. Madame came up the stairs from below, cocking her head inquisitively when she saw me. *"J'attends Ma'amselle Roger,"* I said.

That triggered a burst of French that I had to ask her to repeat. This time she tried her very creaky English. "Ma'amselle 'as a visitor. M'sieur Orsini."

CHAPTER

9

MADAME stood there, smiling, waiting for instructions, so I smiled back and indicated Amy's door. She tapped, and Amy called out, "Who is it?" and Madame gave her the glad tidings in French.

I set my book down and waited while she headed back downstairs. Amy came out the door, looking anxious. She saw me and averted her eyes for a moment, embarrassed. Then Hélène appeared in her own doorway. "Isn't that Victor Orsini downstairs?" she asked.

"Yes. He's here to see me." Amy looked at me nervously. "It's all right. I'll be okay here."

"I know," I said. "Labrosse told me what really happened last year."

Amy bit her lip and said nothing.

Hélène had come down the hall to join her. She had changed into blue jeans and a T-shirt but still looked like something out of *Vogue*. She touched Amy on the arm and spoke to her rapidly. Amy turned and answered also in French, then said to me, "I don't need your judgments."

"Judgment isn't part of my job description. I'm here to keep you safe. Maybe your old buddy downstairs can give us an idea of who's after you."

"Hélène and I will speak to him alone," she said quickly.
"Fine. I'll be right outside."

Amy waited until Hélène joined her, and when they passed me, Hélène put her hand on my arm and smiled. Amy saw the move and flicked a disbelieving glance my way. Did her dishy friend see something in me that she hadn't? I just stood back and let them go ahead.

Hélène led the way into the drawing room, and I was close enough to catch a glimpse of Orsini. He was sitting in an armchair but stood up when they entered. Then Hélène shut the door behind her, and I wandered out of the house toward the front, where Orsini's car was parked.

His driver was right out of a Renoir movie, about my age, chunky, dressed in a dark suit. He had left the car and was leaning against a tree, smoking Gitanes, the pack stuffed into his top pocket. Armand's chauffeur had come around from the back and joined him; they were chatting together like old buddies. It made me wonder whether they were two of a kind, that the wine business was rougher than I'd imagined. Did Armand's chauffeur provide the same kind of muscle for his boss that his buddy did for Orsini?

I took a chair on the terrace, under the awning, and waited, looking as innocent as I could manage. They glanced my way, and the chauffeur said something that made the other guy snort on his cigarette smoke, blowing it out of his nostrils like Puff the Magic Dragon. It figured that they had me marked out as a cream puff, the dumb boyfriend who didn't share their knowledge that Amy and Orsini had been playing Mom and Pop the year before.

After about ten minutes, Orsini came out, with Hélène and Amy beside him. Amy was carrying her purse, she was planning to go with him. I sauntered down toward them, sizing up Orsini. The likeness Cahill had given me was accurate except that the man had preserved his strength in a way the computer couldn't calculate. He was obviously in his late sixties, but he still had a lot of the husky peasant vigor of his youth.

"Going somewhere?" I asked Amy.

"Yes. I'll be gone for a while." She smiled disarmingly.

"Then I'll come with you."

"No." She snapped the word nervously. "No, that won't be necessary."

I smiled back just as brightly. "It could be."

Orsini asked her something in French, and she replied, waving at me. Then it was his turn to smile. He said something else, and Amy translated. "M'sieur Orsini says no."

"I'm working for your uncle, not for Mr. Orsini."

I took another couple of steps toward them, and Orsini snapped his fingers to his chauffeur. It was time to earn my pay.

The chauffeur came for me, moving fast, expecting me to back off and start pleading with Orsini. I could read the pride in his eyes. He would squash me in front of his boss and two attractive women, the stuff that daydreams are made of.

I stood, left foot forward, as if I'd changed my mind in mid-stride. My right hand was down by my groin in case he kicked out. I needn't have worried. He was planning to shoo me away by force of will. He grabbed the lapel of my jacket with his right hand and raised his left forefinger to jab in my face. Reacting to that kind of approach is something you learn in your first hour of hand-to-hand combat. I grabbed his wrist with my right hand, pivoted, and bent down, sending him flying over my head to sprawl on the gravel.

Most fights end there. The thrower stands and waits while the throwee scrambles to his feet and heads for the horizon. This guy had more to prove. He picked himself up and turned, his nose streaming blood. I spoke to Amy over my shoulder. "Tell your buddy to call this guy off before I hurt him."

Amy spoke, but I didn't hear Orsini answer. I flicked a glance around. Everyone else was still where I'd seen them last. I had been half-expecting the Armand chauffeur to butt in, but they were all standing back, so I concentrated on the first one again. He slid his hand into his pocket and came out with a knife. He flicked a button, and it opened with a neat little click. He was about ten feet from me, too far to spring but close enough to posture. He crouched, tossing the knife from hand to hand lightly and smiling. He was good with knives, his stance told me, and my time had come. Behind me I heard one of the women shriek. Out of my own vanity I hoped it was Hélène, anxious for me.

I beamed at the gladiator like a proud father and opened my jacket so he could see the butt of my pistol. *"A bas,"* I said. Down.

He looked at me very hard, his hatred as sharp as the blade of that knife, but after thirty seconds he dropped it. I made a little shooing motion with my hand, backing him off. He did so, walking back with tiny steps until I was able to come forward and pick up the knife.

I shook my head sadly and turned toward the nearest tree. The distance looked right, so I flicked the knife, and sure enough, it turned over three times and stuck into the trunk. To make my point I went after it and bent it sideways until the blade snapped, then tossed it back to its owner.

Finally I turned to Orsini. *"Je vais avec vous."* I'm going with you.

He hadn't seen the gun. As far as he was concerned, I'd done a lion-taming trick, facing down his man through strength of will. On top of which I'd demonstrated that I could handle a knife. Tricks like that impress Corsicans. His face did not change, but he shrugged, and I opened the back door for Amy to get in. Bloody Nose almost ran to the car to open the other back door for Orsini, and then the pair of us got into the front seat.

Orsini was sitting behind his driver, so I turned sideways in my seat to keep an eye on both of them at once. Orsini was looking at me with amusement in his eyes. He continued looking at me as he spoke to Amy in his growly French.

"Mister Orsini wants to know if you would like to work for him," she translated.

It might have been blarney, but I didn't insult him. His driver would be looking for the first chance he got to square accounts. Having Orsini on my side would cut the risks a little. "Tell him I have a job right now. When it's finished, I'll talk to him."

She translated, and he grinned at me, showing yellow teeth. Then he gave the driver an order, and we set off.

I wondered where we were going. Not to an assignation, that was certain. If he'd been planning to replay last summer's date with Amy, she would have taken time to change and pretty up. This had to be business.

After a while I relaxed enough to sit more normally in my seat. It didn't seem likely that Orsini was going to stick a gun in my ear. Amy had probably told him why I was there, which would have amused him. It seemed he was doing her some kind of favor, and I wondered what it was.

From time to time he gave the driver directions, and we wound through a maze of little roads until we came to a house on its own. It was small and had a well-kept flower garden around it. At the edge of the garden was a line of lavender bushes in bloom, outlining the property. Beyond that were vineyards.

The driver pulled in and got out to open Orsini's door. I did the same on my side, opening the door for Amy. "Where are we?" I asked her.

"Raymond Longpré lives here; he's on my list," she said, almost in a whisper.

"You're going to talk to him? After what Labrosse said?"

"Mr. Orsini is with me; that makes it all right." She glared at me. "Don't make things difficult, John. I'm in no danger."

"Fine. I'll wait with the car."

She and Orsini walked up to the door and knocked. A dog woofed inside. It sounded elderly and ill-tempered, but when the door opened, it came out wagging its tail. An old man was with it, and he did a double take when he saw Orsini. But it wasn't fear in his eyes, it was pleasure. They shook hands enthusiastically, and Orsini called to his chauffeur over his shoulder. The man opened the trunk and took out a package, which he carried to Orsini.

Orsini handed it to the old man, and he opened it and smiled, showing the same caliber of dental work I'd noticed on Constance at La Fongeline. He spoke rapidly, gratefully. I caught the word *tabac*. Orsini had brought him something for his pipe. This trip had been planned in advance.

The three of them went into the house, and the chauffeur eyed me warily. He was still angry but was cooling off. He wouldn't try anything; it was fence-mending time. I handed him my handkerchief. *"Pour votre visage."* For your face.

He took it, nodding, and went to crouch beside the outside mirror on the car, spitting on his finger and dabbing at the dried bloodstains with the handkerchief. When he was cleaned up, he stood up and handed it back to me with a curt *"Merci."* Then he took out his cigarettes and proffered them. I smiled and shook my head, stretching my French to explain that I didn't smoke.

There was a bench under an apple tree, and we sat on it side by side, looking out over the sloping vineyards baking gently under the sun. The other guy smoked, and I filled my time wondering why Orsini was doing this for Amy. Was it a first move toward asking her out to a replay of last year's frolic? That didn't seem likely. He was a pimp by profession. He wouldn't bother carrying her books like this. He'd expect to snap his fingers and have her in bed. No, something unexplained was going on, and I wondered what.

By the time my buddy had smoked five cigarettes and was getting restless, Orsini and Amy came out with the old man, who was all smiles and handshakes and kisses on the cheek for her.

She left first, coming to the car, where I joined her. She was rewinding her tape recorder. "So Orsini is helping you with your research. That's friendly," I said.

"More than that. Valuable." She was animated again. "I learned more with him along than I'd ever have got on my own."

"Like what?" I could see Orsini turning away from the door and the chauffeur making a beeline to open it for him.

"Like the fact that Le Loup was real. He really did kill those Germans."

She got into the car, and Orsini joined her. The driver and I got in, and we drove back to the château.

"Are you going out again tonight?" I asked.

"Not tonight, no." It was a careful answer. I read into it that she would be seeing Orsini again. I wondered if she still felt the same attraction to him. And I wondered even more what dear old Eric would say if he could see her now. Behind me, she and Orsini were chatting sporadically, her French too fast and his too heavily accented for me to understand.

When they fell silent, I half turned and asked her, "Can you ask Mr. Orsini a question for me?" My job didn't call for detective work, but I wanted some answers.

"If it's not personal," she said.

"Ask him if he's got any idea who came after you and why?"

"I already did." She sounded smug. "He says he knows the names of the two men but not who sent them. It wasn't him."

"And did you ask who might have killed Pierre?"

"He doesn't know that either."

"And you believe him."

"He's a businessman," she said primly. "I'm sure he does some heavy things when he has to. But he has no reason to kill a historian."

"Does he know who might?"

Before she could answer, Orsini cut in, and she spoke to him first. Then she said, "Mr. Orsini says you ask too many questions."

There was no sense in rocking the boat, so I sat back and enjoyed the ride. Back at the château both Hélène and her father were sitting on the terrace. Hélène stayed put, but Armand walked down to the car and spoke warmly to Orsini, who did not bother getting out of the car. I was reminded of some speakeasy owner trying to win points with Al Capone. Amy got out of the car but stayed there until Armand had finished apple-polishing.

I left them there and walked up to the terrace. Hélène indicated a chair next to her, and I sat. She leaned over and put her hand on my arm. It was the "Hands off, he's mine" signal a high school girl might have used at a dance. I wondered why she was playing the whole thing so broad. In fact, I wondered why I'd been allowed into her boudoir at all. I've had a lot of success with women, but I'm not vain enough to think I'm gorgeous. It was flattering that Hélène had found me suitable to be her sexual partner, but I wasn't going to fool myself that she'd fallen in love with me. She was playing some game. "You were magnificent when that man attacked you," she said, and I just grinned.

She slapped my arm playfully. "Don't be infuriatingly English. You handled the knife like a Corsican. Where did you learn that?"

I gave her the standard army reply. "Long service in bad stations." She laughed out loud. Like most women with good teeth, she had a very melodious laugh. Amy flashed a glance at her and then turned back to the conversation at the car.

After chatting a minute or so, Orsini ended the conversation, his window purred up, and the car pulled away down the drive. Armand stood where he was until it had left the gateway and then came back to the terrace with Amy. His face was like granite. He spoke briefly to Hélène and went inside. Hélène called out something to his back and then waved Amy to a seat. "Was your afternoon well spent?"

"It was wonderful. The old man told me things he never

would have said if Victor hadn't been along." She was working hard at looking enthusiastic, but I could read the uncertainty in her eyes. Why was Hélène making such a show of interest in me? From her attitude toward me earlier I knew she wasn't jealous, yet that was the way she was acting.

Hélène was languid. She didn't overplay her attention to me, but it colored her actions. "And was this information valuable?"

"Yes." Amy had apparently decided to be all business. "It gave me a confirmation that Victor was Le Loup."

Hélène smiled. "With lots of murders, this book of yours could become a bestseller."

"Wouldn't that be neat." Amy threw herself into the role of writer. "The dean and all those stuffy people at U. of T. would hate me, but it wouldn't matter. I'd have the freedom to do what I wanted from here on."

"Is he coming back again?" I asked.

"Tomorrow," Amy said briefly.

"Is he really driving all the way from Marseilles to do this for you?"

Amy frowned angrily. "I don't know why you're so interested in his timetable, but he happens to be in Avignon for a week on business, and he says he can spare the time."

"Fine by me." I stood up. "If you'll excuse me. I have a call to make to Canada. Will that be all right, Hélène?"

"Of course." She waved over her shoulder to the French doors behind her. "Use the phone in the billiard room; it's private."

"Thank you."

I stood up, and as I walked away, Amy called out, "Be sure to give her my love, John." Bitchy, bitchy.

It took me about a minute to explain to the operator whom I was calling and to spell out the number in my lame French. Then the phone rang twice, and Wainwright answered.

"John Locke here, Major."

"Ah, hello, John. How's everything going?"

"It's complicated," I began. "And I thought I should call and get my orders clarified a little."

"In what way complicated?" His words were clipped in that truncated way you get these days when they compress a lot of telephone calls onto a single line. It made him sound irritable.

"The party I was sent here to watch out for showed up today. Seemed very friendly. I had a little trouble with his chauffeur, but that was ironed out, and the party took Amy to see one of her contacts. It was all very civilized."

"You mean you actually met the bounder?" I swallowed my laughter. Nobody has said bounder since 1939.

"Quite the little gentleman. However, there was a complication yesterday. Two men attempted to take our girl for a ride. I stopped them, and the gendarmes have them in custody, but this morning her friend Pierre Armand was terminated, messily."

There was a silence on the line, but I couldn't read anything in it. The same technical efficiency robbed it of all potential for meaning. When he spoke again, he said, "Has the family found out?"

"Yes. We're staying at their château."

"I must contact Pierre's father with condolences," he said, and there was another silence.

"In the meantime, our mutual friend is returning to-morrow for another trip with Amy. He is starting to look

137

harmless here, but I figure someone means her harm or they wouldn't have made a grab at her yesterday. What do you want me to do?"

"Watch her." He rapped it out as he might have done to some mother who allowed her child too close to a fire. "I'm not sure what's happening, but there's no doubt she's in danger. This man we're dealing with is evil. Don't let your guard down."

"Do you have any contacts here who might be able to shed light on any of this? So far I've talked to a Captain Labrosse of the Gendarmerie. He told me a few interesting things, but nothing that puts a face on the man who means her harm."

"Don't be fooled. It's the person I told you about. He may be acting graciously right now, but you know his background." He paused again and added pompously, "Napoleon was Corsican, remember."

"No kidding." He didn't rise to the comment, so I asked the question that had been on my mind from the beginning. "Are you likely to be here on business over the next little while?"

"Not until November, usually," he said. "I try to be there for the Beaujolais Nouveau. But if things are so unusual, I will try to get over for a few days. I'll check my book at the office tomorrow."

"I don't know if there's anything you could do, but I'm sure Amy would be glad to see you."

"How is she?" The affection in his voice was as warm as a hug.

"Shattered by what happened to Pierre. Aside from that, she's professional and distant." I fed him that morsel to soothe his troubled ego. He had probably thought that proximity would have softened Amy toward me and we were double-bedding it by now.

"Tell her I miss her."

"I will, and I'll call again if anything develops."

"Thank you." Another silence and then a burst of concern. "I'm very glad you're there, John. Please take good care of her." I thought he was finished and was waiting for the click of his hanging up, but he added another sentence. "If you're forced to take extraordinary measures, you will be compensated." And then he hung up.

I did the same at my end, frowning at the telephone. What did he mean by extraordinary measures? Was he promising a bonus if I had to kill somebody? Like Orsini, for instance?

I went back out. The women had become chummier in my absence and were talking animatedly. They stopped and looked up as I approached.

"How is she?" Amy asked.

"Eric send his regards and wants me to say he misses you."

"Eric? Wainwright?" Hélène looked surprised. "Amy has lost her bet, John. She told me you would be calling your *petite amie*."

"That situation is vacant." I sat down in the same chair and watched Amy regrouping for another attack. Dammit, the woman was jealous. She didn't want me, but she was angry at Hélène's taking over.

"You mean that Janet is only a neighbor?" She asked it teasingly, but the claws were out.

"And friend," I said, "But I think a lawyer would describe it as an arm's-length friendship. We like the same kind of music."

Hélène grabbed the lifeline and hauled the conversation back out of dangerous waters. "And what kind of music is that?"

"Baroque mostly."

"Not rock?" Amy had realized she was getting out of line and was apologizing to Hélène with the question.

"No. I guess I burned my ears out on the stuff when I was a teenager." Not the real answer. I don't like rock music because it's overpowered by the bass line. I think the beat of a piece of music should be like the shell of a pie, supporting the structure, not the main ingredient. But they didn't want my philosophy. They wanted to talk, and soon Amy lapsed into French, so I excused myself and took a walk around the grounds, assessing each of the windows on the second floor the way a sniper would.

Being on my own gave me chance to do some thinking. On top of the major problems of the day, I was concerned about a couple of smaller things, both of them involving Hélène. To start with, why was she so dry-eyed about her brother's murder? Her father was shattered, but she was showing no more concern than she would have for a dead dog on the highway. And secondly, why had she volunteered the dance of the seven veils for me? Hell, she had to have guys waiting in line, rich men, movie stars, you name it. Did she prefer what must have looked like rough trade? Or was she more deeply affected by Pierre's death than she had let on and had taken the consolation of the nearest pair of arms? Baffling.

The women went in after a while, and I followed, heading up to my room, picking up my book from the second landing. I expected to be on guard all night outside Amy's room, so I took the opportunity to grab a catnap. Then I showered and changed my shirt and jacket and headed back down to the billiard room to wait for dinner.

There was a full-sized table there, and I set up the billiard balls and spent a mindless half hour practicing cannons. At one point, the eldest of the children of the house timidly stuck his head into the room. He was nine or so, and I figured he played in here whenever the Armands were away and his mother's back was turned. I waved him in and played him a couple of games. By the time we'd finished, his brother and two sisters were sitting watching us like the three wise monkeys.

At seven, Amy came in for me. "Hélène father isn't having dinner. We were planning to go into town."

"Fine." The kid was ahead at that point. He would be a real shark by the time he reached his teens. I told him we were going and gravely handed him ten francs. Not a fortune, but his eyes lit up, and then he timidly refused it. I winked at him and stuck it into his shirt pocket. I like kids.

We drove to Vaison-la-Romaine and had an excellent dinner at the same restaurant where Orsini had made his move on Amy the year before. Nothing out of the ordinary happened, and we were back by ten-thirty.

Hélène suggested a nightcap, but Amy demurred. She was tired, jet lag, she explained, but I figured she was grieving for Pierre. That was when Hélène made her announcement.

"I have been thinking about what John said about the window in your room," she said. "I think you should have my room, and I'll take yours. Nobody will come after me." Madame was passing the door as she spoke, but Hélène ignored her. As far as I was concerned, it was risky now.

This ruse would only work if nobody knew about it except us three.

Amy protested, but not for long. She was obviously drained from the day's unhappiness, and she wanted to sleep. I went up with them and moved her stuff into Hélène's room.

Then Hélène and I went back down to the drawing room and had a cognac. She didn't say or do anything to reflect what had happened in her room earlier that day, so I held my tongue and enjoyed the drink. At eleven, she stood up and yawned. "Come on," she said. She went upstairs, and I followed her. I'd made up my mind to stay outside her door. As far as any outsider was concerned, this was still Amy's room, and somebody might come in there looking for her. That they found a beautiful blonde instead of a striking brunette would not stop the average sensual hood from doing something naughty. I had to be on hand.

When she reached her door, she turned. "Where are you going?"

"Nowhere. I'll be out here if anything happens."

She smiled a deep-down smile and said, "But how can anything happen if you are outside?" She pushed the door open and indicated that I was to enter.

I went in and quickly cased the room. Nobody was hiding anywhere. I turned to tell her this, but she was already half-undressed, moving with the practiced speed she would have used if she had been alone, not attempting to get my hormones tap-dancing.

She stripped and slipped into bed, naked, then patted the bed beside her. I can take a hint. I quickly stripped, putting my clothes over a chair where I could find them in the dark if I had to. Then I switched off the light and quietly slipped my pistol from its holster and pushed it under the pillow.

Our lovemaking was slower this time, more like an old married couple than two virtual strangers. She was controlled, making no attempt to try anything athletic. When it was over, she slipped her hand into mine and started talking, very softly, so that I had to keep my ear almost against her lips to hear her. It was all very romantic, right up to the moment when she told me she wanted me to kill Orsini.

CHAPTER

10

THAT was when the other shoe finally dropped and I understood why she had whisked me off to bed so promptly. She had me figured for a killer. She needed this little job of tidying up done and had figured she could get it done for free, if you didn't count the wear and tear, by rolling me in the hay, making me feel that she was wild for me, and bingo, I'd take all her worries away.

When I didn't answer for about a minute, she started the soft sell, squirming closer to me, kissing my ear. "Will you do it?" she whispered.

I had to be cagey. If I got on my high horse, she would holler rape. Nobody would take my word over hers. Beautiful women are pure as the driven snow. I'd be inside a French jail before I could get my pants on. "What has he done that I must kill him for you?"

"He murdered my brother," she said. As the Brits would say, that was a load of cobblers. She didn't care about her brother. She had some other reason for wanting Orsini dead. But I played along, the personification of sweet reason. "How can you be sure? If he'd done that, he would never have come here today like he did."

She spoke softly, placating me. "You are a soldier, John, a man of action. A good man. He is a Corsican."

"Well, if you're certain he's done it, let's go to the gendarmes and have him arrested." I took pains to sound as if I were working things out, not pleading with her. I had to seem strong and as close to silent as I could; otherwise, I'd be on the outs. With this bird of prey, that could be downright dangerous. Ask Orsini.

"You're not afraid?" a teasing question.

"Not of him, no. But I'm a bodyguard. I don't go around killing people unless they're trying to kill me."

She changed gears, leaving her problem alone for a while, cranking up the charm instead. "John, you are precious to me. This has never happened to me, not to see a man and know he is the one. You are the very first."

Maybe if I watched the soaps I'd be ready for dialogue like that. I played along, anyway. "And you are very dear to me, Hélène. But if something goes wrong and the police find what I have done, I won't see you again." Ever, probably; they still use the guillotine on murderers in France.

"Nothing can go wrong. We will do it together. I have a plan." Her voice was pure syrup, but her pacing made me sure she'd worked out every move before she undid that first button on her blouse.

"How?" I kissed her, high on the forehead, and stroked her flank, the besotted swain, ready to leap tall buildings, even with a rope around my neck.

"When he comes tomorrow to visit Amy, I will invite him to an assignation. He will come. He is vain, that one."

"And then, while you're blowing in one ear, I'll stick my gun in the other?"

She slapped me playfully, but I could feel her spine stiffening. She was getting impatient. "You will find a way."

"And then what? When he is dead, you will thank me and go away." I said it wistfully, as if I didn't know for a dead certainty that was the program.

"Then we will be together always." Not a whisper of marriage. Either she didn't believe in the institution or she thought I didn't and didn't want to make me gun-shy. "We could have a wonderful life. You will love Paris. We will live there and travel together and spend all our nights like this." Not a bad idea, except I wondered how many of them would be spent planning murders.

"I must think about this."

She was silent for a moment, and then her hands began to move. "No. You must think about this," she said, and I did.

Half an hour later she was asleep. She had made love to me ferociously, as if she were either mad for my body or extremely skillful at what she was doing. I figured it was the latter, but I've always enjoyed watching experts at work, and afterward she didn't bother doing any more selling. She just said, "We will make our plan in the morning," confident that she'd burned out any resistance I might have harbored.

When I was certain she wasn't likely to wake up, I slipped out of bed and got dressed. As far as Orsini was concerned, this was still Amy's room, and somebody might make a move on it. I didn't want to greet them in the altogether. When I had my clothes and shoes on, I sat on the floor beside the bed with my back to the wall, watching the window.

I was drowsing when he came. The scraping on the roof alerted me, and I stood up silently and moved away from the bed, staying opposite the window, waiting for a man's shape to grow against the square of grayness.

Hélène was a fresh-air freak, and the window was open about two feet. He didn't even have to raise it. He slithered through like a snake, silently taking his weight on his hands and drawing his legs in after him.

I let him advance toward the bed. My night vision was clearer than his; he was used to the starlight outside. I'd been sitting in darkness for three hours. I saw him approach the bed and raise a pistol. Without waiting, I put a bullet into his shoulder, high up.

He screamed in pain and surprise and fell sideways. I heard his gun clatter to the floor and then Hélène's own scream. I clicked on the light. "Stay down," I said, and she squeezed herself under the pillows. I walked over the bed and looked down at the guy on the floor. He was holding his injured shoulder in his left hand, he eyes wide with pain and horror. His gun was a yard away from him, but he made no attempt to go for it, didn't even look at me. He had suddenly realized that pain hurts.

I stepped down and kicked the gun farther away from him and then tapped his left elbow with my toe. He looked up at me owlishly, like a drunk. It was Armand's chauffeur. "Okay, Hélène, ask him who sent him."

She sat up, wrapping the sheet around her. If the chauffeur hadn't been in shock, he would have been exhilarated, for her body was tightly outlined under the sheet, her nipples standing out like the winner in a wet T-shirt contest. She hissed at him in French, and he said nothing, just looked at her, then at me.

I lowered my pistol and pointed it between his eyes. "Tell him he's got ten seconds or I blow his brains out."

He didn't need a translation. He babbled for mercy, but she shut him up curtly and repeated her question, and his answer poured out.

"He says he met a man in the village. The man offered him ten thousand francs to kill Amy. He doesn't know the man."

I laughed. "Tell him he watches too much television. I need the man's name. Ask if it was the guy you don't like."

"I have a better idea," she said savagely, and came around the bed to kick him hard in the injured shoulder before I could stop her.

He screeched in pain, and behind her the door burst open, and Armand almost tumbled in, followed by Amy. They all babbled at one another too fast for me to follow, and Armand came around the bed and saw who was lying there. He gasped, and I saw him clutch his chest. Lord. That was all we needed, a heart attack now. "Get your father's pills," I snapped, and Hélène let her sheet drop as she sat him down gently on the bed and took the vial from his dressing-gown pocket. She put one under his tongue, and he whispered something.

"D'accord, Papa." She grabbed her sheet and scooped up her clothes and headed for a screen in the far corner of the room.

Amy was looking at me, seeming to be more concerned that I had seen Hélène nude than the fact that this man had been in the room with a gun. "He came to kill you," I said, improvising quickly. "I heard him come into the room and saw he had a gun, so I stopped him. He says he met a man in the village who offered him ten thousand francs to shoot you."

"Me? Why?"

"With luck we're going to find out." I picked up his pistol. It was a neat little Beretta .32, plenty big enough to do the job he'd come for. I slipped the magazine out and worked the action. He had a shell up the spout, and

I caught it as it flew out and put it and the magazine in my pocket. "If there's a phone on this floor, call the gendarmes. Tell them what's happened."

"On this floor?" She was bewildered and fluttery, more so than she had been when we found Pierre's body.

"They may have other guys downstairs; they could see you through a window and finish this."

Hélène came out from behind the screen, wearing her jeans and top, barefoot. "I'll go," she said.

Armand spoke. "No." It was a painful whisper. "No gendarmes. We will end this here."

"This guy needs a hospital." Armand had lots of clout, I knew that much, but he was about to break the law, and I could end up taking the fall for it. I'd pulled the trigger.

"Wait outside," he whispered, and waved at the two women. They went, Hélène moving confidently, Amy backing out, not knowing what was about to happen here but afraid.

When she had gone, Armand smiled at me shyly, like a new recruit. "We will find out who sent him," he said, and asked the man a question.

The guy answered rapidly. I made out the word *blessé*, wounded. It didn't soften Armand's heart. "Kick him," he told me.

The guy was in agony. I could see that. My bullet had shattered his upper arm and penetrated his side. Probably it had stopped against his ribs. He was hurting like he'd never hurt before, but he wasn't about to die. I kicked him lightly on the sole of the left foot. He hissed with the jolt, but he could handle it. "Tell him the next kick is on his wound," I instructed, and Armand did it, then repeated his question in a slow voice.

He answered, speaking fast, apologetically.

Armand turned to me. "As I thought. He was working for Dubois, the man you fought today."

"That means he was working for Orsini," I said.

Armand put the question, and the man shook his head. It must have hurt him not being able to shrug, but his shrugging days were on hold until that shoulder healed.

Armand repeated the question, and this time the man agreed. I could tell by the tone.

"Shoot him," Armand told me.

"No." I put my gun in its holster. "I'm a bodyguard. I did my job, and I can support that. I don't shoot wounded men."

I'd tossed the chauffeur's empty gun on the bed, and Armand picked it up. "I will do it myself," he said, and pointed it at the man's head.

The man babbled and covered his face as Armand pulled the trigger. It clicked, and Armand swore, dropped the gun, and flopped back on the pillows, exhausted. "Get my daughter."

I went to the door. Hélène was in the corridor with Amy. "Your father wants you."

She came into the room, and he gave her an order in rapid French. She nodded and left. "What did he say?" I asked Amy, who was still holding on to the door frame. She was wearing a white nylon nightdress and looked delicious. That she was bewildered and not so much in charge as usual didn't hurt a bit.

"He asked her to get the doctor from the village." She hesitated a moment and then put a question shakily. "John, what's going on?"

"He came to shoot you." She trembled, and I caught her by the elbow. She came into my arms like a baby, trying to make herself safe. I held her tight, patting her shoulder rhythmically. "He was sent by the man who drives Orsini's car," I said. "You've got to leave this place, Amy. Go back home where you're safe."

She didn't reply, just stood there, warm against my chest, shaking. "Come on," I said after a moment. "Get your dressing gown on. You're freezing."

At my urging she turned and walked slowly down the hallway to her room. I waited at the open door while she put on her housecoat and turned to face me. She was pale but had stopped trembling. "Why is all this happening?" she asked in a whisper.

"I'm not sure, but it's not about you. Not just about you, anyway. I'm sure of that." It probably didn't matter, anyway. When news of my shooting somebody reached Labrosse, he would ship both me and Amy home, at the least. The alternative wasn't worth thinking about, that he would charge me with wounding and sling me in jail. I wanted the ten grand this assignment would earn me, but not enough to do hard time for it.

"There is something going on," she said softly. "M'sieur Armand has a serious hate going for Victor. I could tell from his face when they met outside this afternoon. He was polite, but he was angry."

I didn't answer. I was beginning to realize they were in trouble. Hélène wanted Orsini dead, and yet she didn't seem to care for her brother at all. The way I was reading it, Orsini was trying to muscle into the family business and take it over. I got back to my own business. "Will you be all right here for a minute? I have a feeling Armand is liable to start kicking the guy I shot."

"Yes. I'm going to get dressed, and I'll join you."

"Don't go anywhere without telling me. There could be

somebody else outside waiting for you. You're in danger, Amy."

"All right." Her voice was dull. Her worry circuits were all overloaded. I gave her a cheerful thumbs up and went back to the other bedroom. There was no problem with the wounded man, but Armand was in distress, trying to take another pill. I took the bottle from him and shook out a pill and gave it to him. He put it under his tongue without acknowledgment and lay back.

I leaned against the wall and waited for the women to return. Hélène arrived first, trotting down the corridor from her father's bedroom. "The doctor is coming," she told me.

"Good. Before he comes, tell me. Where did your dad find this guy? He looked like a hood to me when I saw him on the street. Did you hire him for protection, or what?"

"He was recommended to us."

"By whom? It wasn't the local bishop!"

She didn't answer at once. I watched her beautiful face, almost able to see the wheels turning inside her head. At last she said, "I have not told you everything, John." I said nothing and after a pause she looked at her father, then at me, and made a slight beckoning motion with her head. I followed her out the door, and she said, "Orsini is trying to force us out of the business. He has some kind of hold over Papa. He is the one who insisted we hire this man as protection."

"Protection from whom? It sounds as if the only problem around here is Orsini. Having his man in the family is like inviting the fox into the henhouse."

She shrugged. "Do not ask me why. Papa does not tell

me everything. I know only that Orsini must be killed."

She didn't add anything, just looked at me, her face pale but still stunningly beautiful. I could read in her glance a tacit repetition of the question she had asked me in bed. Would I kill Orsini. It was appealing to hear the truth like this, although it still didn't make me want to jump on a white horse and rush off to slay her personal dragon, but I reached out and patted her arm reassuringly. "Everything's going to be fine."

There was the noise of a car outside. "That will be the doctor," she said, and left. I waited there while she went downstairs and came back with an elderly man carrying a medical bag. He went over to the injured man, but Hélène spoke rapidly to him, and he turned to her father first. He took his pulse and listened to his heart, then took his blood pressure. He said something to Hélène and she turned to me. "The doctor says Papa should be in bed. Will you carry him, John?"

"Sure." She spoke to her father, and I picked him up. He wasn't very heavy, and I carried him in my arms down the corridor to his own room, laying him on the bed and covering him. He lay back and shut his eyes, and I went back down the hall to watch the doctor work. There was a syringe on the top of his bag, and the chauffeur was lying flat, his eyes closed. The doctor had raised his injured arm and cut away his shirt. He was digging into the smaller wound under his arm. He brought out the flattened bullet and held it up, looking at me fiercely but saying nothing.

Hélène caught the glance and spoke to him sharply, picking up the guy's pistol and waving it. The doctor shrugged and laid the bullet and his tweezers aside and dressed the wound under the arm. Then he turned his attention to the shattered arm, tutting sharply and speaking to Hélène again in rapid French. She answered, and he bound up the arm and gave the man another injection.

At last he stood up, and he and Hélène talked for a while. Then she translated for me. "He is going home to get a proper splint for Torrance. I have said we will put him in his room and hire a nurse to take care of him. Can you get him back to his room?"

"Sure. Can you show me the way?"

I picked the man up over my left shoulder in a fireman's carry. The doctor stood aside, and Hélène led me out of the room and downstairs. The factor of the business was awake, peeking out of the kitchen, but Hélène spoke sharply to him, and he closed the door as we went out through the back door. I drew my pistol and dangled it in my right hand as we crossed the yard and climbed the stairs to Torrance's apartment over the garage. It was a big, comfortable room, but he lived in it like a pig. There were clothes everywhere, and the bed had not been made for days by the look of it. Hélène hissed and pointed to a chair. "Set him down."

I dropped him on the chair and waited while she quickly changed the linen on the bed, finding what she needed in a cupboard at the top of the stairs. She seemed so familiar with the place that part of my mind niggled at the thought that she may have tried her charms on the chauffeur at some time. Anything seemed possible on a crazy night like this.

I took the man's clothes off and put him between the sheets. She had filled a water jug, and she set it and a glass on the table next to the bed. "Right. He will live," she said. "I will wait here for the doctor to return. You go back to Amy."

I made my way back to the house. I was looking all

around but I saw nobody anywhere. The factor of the property must have gone back to bed, because there were no lights on the ground floor and no sound. As I went upstairs, the doctor came down. He looked at me without speaking, and I stood aside for him. It looked like he had me pegged for dumb muscle, hurting poor innocent Frenchmen for no reason except a paycheck.

The light was on in the room where the shooting had happened, and Amy was in there, dressed in blue jeans and a T-shirt, sitting on the bed. I joined her, and she said, "I don't know what to do, John."

"The smart thing would be to leave. There's a whole gang war going on here. Orsini is being charming to you by day, but he sent a man to kill you tonight. Now that he's failed, he may come out of his closet and try harder tomorrow. We should clear out."

She looked at me sightlessly, staring into the space behind my head. At last she said, "I'm going to phone Eric in Toronto."

It seemed like the best bet. I had no doubt he would reinforce what I'd said and we'd be on our horse by morning. "Okay, the phone's in the billiard room."

She got up like a sleepwalker and went downstairs. I went with her and sat on a couch, listening while she phoned. Surprisingly, she spoke to him in French. To keep the conversation private, I guessed.

At last she said, "*D'accord. Au 'voir*, Eric." Her tone was soft; she sounded like a lover.

When she turned around, she said, "Eric is coming over. He's taking the Concorde from New York. He'll be here tomorrow."

"Unless he's bringing a bag of money to buy Orsini off

or a company of Gurkhas to hunt him down, forget it. His presence isn't going to make any difference."

"He says I should go back to Constance's. Not to tell anyone where I'm going, just get back there and wait for him."

"And you're going to?"

She tightened her face like an angry child. "I have no choice."

"You mean he pulls the strings and you move. Is that it?"

"No, that's not it." I thought she was going to stamp her foot with exasperation. "That's not it at all. But that's what I'm going to do. Okay?"

My job was to guard her, not guide her, so I stood up and waited for her to move. Outside I saw a car pull up in the driveway and pass the house, heading directly for the garage. The doctor, coming back to attend to his patient. "Go up and pack. I'm going to see that everything's okay with the guy I shot. I'll tell Hélène that you're heading back to Paris."

"Fine." She walked briskly out of the room and across to the stairway. I switched off the light and slipped out of the French doors and around the side to the garage. I don't know why I didn't go through the house and out the back door, but if it was divine guidance, then I ought to spend more time in church. The car was not the doctor's little Renault that I'd seen at the side door earlier. It was a Mercedes, and a man was standing beside it smoking a cigarette.

I waited in the darkness beside the house, and then I heard a commotion on the stairs leading up to the chauffeur's room. I could make out Hélène's voice, breathless and angry. It sounded as if she were being forced downstairs, probably by somebody with an arm around her throat.

The smoker beside the car took one last drag, then dropped the cigarette and put his foot on it. I didn't hesitate. I drew my gun and ran up to him before he could turn around properly. He was half-facing me when I got there, and I clouted him with the butt of the gun on the side of the jaw. He gasped and dropped, and I caught him and laid him down, then took his place beside the car, keeping my foot on his throat.

I had been right. Another man came down the stairs, struggling with Hélène. He thought I was his partner and called out to me in a low voice. I grunted something and came forward as if to help him. It was dark, and he was busy enough with Hélène that he didn't catch on to his mistake. I stepped up beside him as if to help and slammed him in the temple with the butt of the pistol. It didn't drop him, but he released Hélène and staggered, and I kicked him hard in the knee and clubbed him on the back of the neck, putting a lot of follow-through into it. He collapsed without a sound.

"Now we call the gendarmes," I said. "You've got a cast-iron case."

"No." It was a command. "This one saw Torrance. He will tell the gendarmes, and it will be you who is in trouble."

That made sense, and I didn't argue. "What do we do instead?"

"You know the road outside Faucon?"

"Yes. You mean where it drops off into the ravine on the east side?"

"We will put them in the car and push them off there."

She said it in the tone of voice she might have used to tell her dressmaker to raise the hemline an inch.

"Whoa." I held up one hand. "That's murder."

"And what do you think they were going to do with me?" Her question was contemptuous.

"That's not a defense for cold-blooded murder. I've spoken to Labrosse. He's a good cop, he'd find out what happened. Probably wouldn't have to work to do it. Torrance would tell him, and if he didn't, Orsini would. We can't do it, Hélène. What's your second choice?"

"Get rid of them."

"I'll get Amy. We're driving back to Paris. She wants to go home. I'll put her on the plane and then come back here."

She grabbed my arm. "How can I be sure you will? How do I know you won't get on the plane with her?"

"You have my word on it."

Before she could answer, one of the men groaned. I stooped to check him. It was the first one I'd stopped. He was coming around. His mouth was filled with blood. I guessed his jaw was broken. He wouldn't be much of a threat, but I searched him, anyway. He had a switchblade in his left sock, no gun. Then I searched the other one. He had a pistol as well as a knife. I jammed all the weapons into my pockets, then removed their belts and tore the support buttons and the zippers out of their pants. It's an old Gypsy trick. It meant they would need one hand at all times to keep their pants up. That plus their injuries would stop them from getting belligerent.

"Go and help Amy down with her bags. Leave mine in the room."

"You do it. I'll stay here."

She may have been protesting my chauvinism or more

likely looking for a chance to stick a knife in both guys. Either way, I couldn't risk it. "If we're going to work together, we have to divide the job properly," I said. "Go and help her down to the car. I'll get these guys out of sight before the doctor comes back and sees them."

"All right." She left, crunching away across the gravel to the back door. I tumbled the two men into the rear seat of the car and drove it into a vacant stall in the garage, next to the car I'd hired. I sat there with the lights out and waited. After a while a small car drove up. I watched it in the mirror and saw the doctor get out. He said something brisk under his breath and then took his bag and climbed to the apartment over the garage. I slipped out and over to the back door of the house, thankful that Torrance was such a lousy housekeeper. The doctor would not make out the signs of the struggle Hélène had put up.

I was worried that the women would come downstairs and alert him, but he'd left before they appeared, so I went back to the car and waited. The man with the broken jaw had come to, and he sat up groggily when I opened the door, then groaned and mumbled something in French. Probably telling me his jaw hurt. I opened the door a fraction so that the roof light came on and he stared at me incredulously. "Siddown," I told him loud and clear, the way my mother speaks to foreigners. It worked. He sat back in the seat, spitting into his handkerchief.

A minute later, the women came out. I got out of the car and put the bags into the trunk. Amy asked, "Why isn't yours here?"

"I'm coming back. I'll explain later. You're going to drive the rental car. I'll follow in this one. Make your way to some really quiet road. I'll flash my lights, and you stop while I dump these guys."

"What will you do with them?" Hélène asked.

"I've already done it. They're hurt, and they can't run. I'll take the car keys away and leave them. It will be morning before they get word to their boss. By that time I'll be back."

"Do not forget." Her voice had a husky edge to it, like the heroine in *A Man and a Woman*. It may have fooled Amy, but I took it in stride.

"You have my word."

She stood on tiptoe and kissed me passionately. I heard Amy gasp in surprise, but it was a good kiss, so I let it run its course, then said, *"A demain."* Until tomorrow. Hell, I've seen as many French movies as the next guy.

Hélène stood back and then hugged Amy and said something rapid in French. Amy answered, and I said, "Okay, let's go. Remember, we want them off the track. Lead off in a different direction to the one we'll end up going. Got that?"

"Yes," Amy said tartly. I gave her the car keys, and she got in and started it up, noisily. I patted Hélène on the arm and got into the Mercedes. Amy backed out, and I followed her down the driveway and out to the left, the opposite direction from our real destination.

She drove for fifteen minutes, turning off at last onto a winding road that didn't seem wide enough to accommodate a car coming the other way. After about a mile she slowed, and I flashed the lights. She stopped, and I did and took the keys out of the ignition. I opened the door and turned to check the two men. Broken Jaw had recovered as much as he would without dental surgery, and the other one was awake. I pulled his head toward me and checked the pupils of his eyes. They were both the same size, a good indication that he wasn't concussed. He stared into my eyes as I checked him, but I don't think he was registering any features. He was wondering how his plan could have come unstuck so easily. I patted him on the shoulder. "She'll be right." It's an Aussie expression too colloquial for any shreds of English he might have known, but I was sure he would be okay, so I got out and walked ahead to join Amy in the other car. As I got into it, I tossed the Mercedes ignition keys over the low hedge. Nobody would find them in a year. More problems for the lads.

She said nothing, still dwelling on Hélène's fond farewell. I sat back and let her get on with the driving, not speaking.

After a few minutes she asked, "How come you said you'd be going back?"

"Hélène thinks you're leaving the country. I promised her that I wouldn't. Once you're installed with Eric, I can sort it all out."

"Why would you lie to her?" The cold, hard voice of jealousy.

"Security," I said. "Your security."

She was silent for another mile or two, then said, "That was some kiss she gave you."

"I'd just saved her from a fate worse than death. Those two guys were not planning to discuss existentialism with her before they killed her."

She said no more, just drove, a little too aggressively, all the way to La Fongeline. There were no lights on, and Amy drove right to the parking spot at the back door. She opened the door briskly and slid sideways to get out. I reached over to check her, and she looked at me angrily. "What is it?"

"I don't like it," I said. "Her dog isn't barking."

CHAPTER

11

AMY didn't answer, but in the light from the car interior I could see she was trembling. I took out the gun I'd found on the second man at the garage and checked it. It was an old .38 Colt revolver, loaded in all six cylinders. Like most revolvers, it had no safety catch. "Shut the door," I told her.

She pushed the door closed very quietly, and I came around the car and gave her the pistol. "All you do is point and pull the trigger. Can you do that?"

"Yes," she whispered.

"Good. Come with me." I led her over to the woodpile, first checking all around it to see nobody was hiding there. "Crouch here and wait for me. I'm going to take a look around."

"Okay." Another whisper. I patted her arm and left, walking along the east side of the house, toward the dog run. I could smell blood, and I moved slowly, pulling out my little lithium penlight. It's small but powerful, similar to the one I'd carried in the army. I cut down the beam by holding it behind my clenched fingers, letting only a sliver of light escape. One flash told the story. The dog's throat had been cut.

I doused the light and went back to the wall of the house, easing my way around it to the south side. The moon was gone by now—the deep darkness of predawn had settled— but I knew my silhouette against the French doors at the south side would be a target if there was someone inside, so I did things by the numbers, almost lying down, reaching up with one hand to shove my poor overused Visa card in against the lock. It gave, and I opened the door and crept into the big room, keeping low.

There was no sound, but I crouched for long seconds, listening, before I flicked on my light, holding it at the extreme stretch of my left arm so that a viewer would have thought I was a yard away from my real position. The room was as I remembered, nothing out of place except for a bundle of rags in front of the couch.

I stood up and took another pace forward. The bundle of rags was the tiny body of Constance, lying with her head canted awkwardly to the left. Whoever had killed her had not bothered to use a knife. He had broken her frail old neck like a dry twig.

Kneeling, I put one finger on the pulse in the throat, but it was gone. All the intellect and wisdom of nearly eighty years had been snuffed out by some unlettered thug from the slums of Marseilles.

I was ready to kill whoever had done it, but I carried on, as I would have done if a comrade in arms had been killed, checking the house room by room, making sure nobody was hiding and making equally sure that I didn't leave any fingerprints.

When I was certain the killer had gone, I went back out the way I'd entered, pulling the door closed behind me. My mind was racing as I walked back around to the woodpile. We should call the gendarmes. They would come and investigate thoroughly, perhaps finding some clue that would lead directly to the killer. But while they did that they would also ship Amy and me out of the country. In fact, it could be worse than that. Labrosse could lock us up for complicity. And whatever he found would not change the fact that Orsini had done this, probably before he came calling on Amy this afternoon. He had come here looking for her, had found us gone, and had tortured Constance to find out where we were, then killed her.

I gave a low whistle and called, "Amy."

She stood up, against the woodpile. "What did you find? What's the matter with the dog?"

"Nothing. I guess he recognized my smell; Constance had told him I was a friend. I figure we should move in upstairs and talk to her in the morning."

"Should we knock on the door? She's probably asleep." The reasonable question.

"At her age she needs any sleep she can get. Leave it. If she comes out, she'll see the car and know we're back. Come on, let's go in."

"Okay." She came forward and handed me back the gun. "I'm glad I didn't have to use this thing. It's scary just handling it."

"Takes training." My voice was grim, and I saw her head turn toward me in surprise at the tone.

"Are you all right?" She was almost solicitous.

"Just whacked out. I'm OD'd on fights this last few hours."

She went to the back of the car and unlocked the trunk, not speaking. I hoisted out the bigger of her two bags and carried it up the short stone stairway to the door of the upper apartment. It was locked, but the same Visa card opened it in two seconds, and I went in and turned on the light.

Amy followed, and I carried her bag up to the second floor, with her just behind me. "I'll catch a nap on the couch. You rest up. We've got a big day tomorrow."

She looked at me oddly. "In what way big?"

I was thinking of a showdown with Orsini but couldn't put that card on the table, so I said, "Eric's coming. You'll want to be ready to see him, rested up, I don't know." I waved one hand vaguely. "Give me a break, Amy. I need some rest, too. I haven't been to bed yet."

She looked at me oddly, weighing the words against the kiss she'd seen Hélène deliver. "No," she said at last. "I'd forgotten that. Will you be all right downstairs?"

"Dandy." I gave her a grin and went back down to the main room, where I put the lights out and wedged a chair under the doorknob before curling up on the couch.

I was more tired than I'd thought and didn't wake up until after daybreak, when Amy came downstairs again to hit the shower. She seemed bright and cheerful and said, "Good morning," in a happy half yodel. I got the feeling she was glad to be away from Hélène and the unhappiness of the Armand house.

"You're bright-eyed and bushy-tailed," I said. "Good morning yourself. I'll get some coffee going."

"Great." She sailed on into the bathroom. I splashed some water on my face at the kitchen sink and washed my hands, then found the coffee. Fortunately, Constance hadn't cleaned out the food we'd put in the fridge. We had milk, and there was cereal still in the cupboard. I set things out for breakfast and got the coffee started. When Amy came out of the bathroom, I went in and showered. I would have liked to shave, but my razor was still at the Armands'. I'm fair-haired enough that my beard doesn't start looking scrungy until the second day, so I washed vigorously and came out feeling a little readier for action.

Amy was in blue jeans and a T-shirt that was obviously French. It had flowers on it instead of some dumb message. She was sitting at the table with the coffeepot and the cereal in front of her, and we ate breakfast.

"What are you planning? Just wait here for Eric?"

"I think that's best." She was still bright, and I got the impression of a lover waiting for her other half. What she and Wainwright had going was important to her.

"He probably won't be here until late. The Concorde flies from New York to Paris; then he'll have to change planes for Marseilles and drive up. We'll be here all day."

She looked up inquisitively over her cereal. "Does that bother you?"

"Just so long as you don't go talking to people. Labrosse will hear about it, and we'll have trouble. Perhaps Eric has contacts with the Gendarmerie and can ease things for you."

"Perhaps he does." She smiled. "Why so suddenly law-abiding, John? Hélène told me what you did to those two men. That was hardly legal."

"That was a response to an attack. Attacks put all the normal rules on hold."

She half-smiled but said nothing. And then I heard a car coming up the drive. We went to the back window and saw a big Citroën making its way slowly over the ruts. I slipped my jacket on to cover my gun and put the Colt revolver into my right-hand pocket.

"Stay here." I whisked out the door and down the steps, covering the half-dozen paces to the woodpile before the car came around the corner of the house. I crouched behind the logs, waiting until the car stopped. There were two men in it. I didn't recognize the driver, but the other was Eric Wainwright. He got out of the car and spoke in French to his driver. He called him by name, I got that much, and the name he used was Chrétien.

I came out from behind the logs, moving like a man who's been out for a morning stroll. "Good morning, Major. How are you?"

"John?" He looked surprised for a moment, then stuck out his hand. "How are you, and how's Amy?"

"Come on and see for yourself. We were just having breakfast when we saw the car."

He cocked his head to one side. "And you came down? Very good. Very professional indeed."

"A lot's been happening." I led him toward the steps to the apartment. "Amy will fill you in." I was thinking as we walked. It was impossible for him to have flown from Canada in such a short time. That meant he must have been in France. And yet she had called his number in Toronto and spoken to him herself the night before. Call forwarding, I supposed; I'm ignorant of most technology except where it directly affects my work. Could it shunt a call to Canada and back without the caller's noticing? And in any case, why had he lied?

Any doubts I'd had about his relationship with Amy were swept away by her greeting. She kissed him full on the lips and hugged him. "Eric, what a wonderful surprise! John was just saying you'd be late today."

"Ah, these days anything is possible if you're prepared to pay the price," he said.

It wasn't a full answer, but she didn't need one. She was hanging on to his arm and steering him to the table. "Have some coffee."

"That would be lovely." He sat down, and she fussed with another cup. "Oh, John. Would you be so kind as to call Chrétien, please. He could use some of this as well."

"Sure." I went down to the car. Chrétien was sitting in the driver's seat and, being a Frenchman, was smoking the inevitable cigarette. "*Café?*" I asked, smiling.

"*Oui, merci.*" He got out and stomped on his cigarette and followed me back upstairs. I was sizing him up as he moved. Around forty, compact and slope-shouldered, what a boxing trainer would describe as a useful build, long reach. I wondered whether Eric had retained him solely for his driving skills, or was he under the same kind of pressures as the Armands? Was that why he had offered me a bonus for some unspecified action? Perhaps for killing Orsini? As Alice in Wonderland has it, "Curiouser and curiouser."

When the driver and I got upstairs, Amy chatted to the man as she gave him coffee, but she suspended her conversation with Wainwright. As soon as Chrétien had finished, Wainwright sent him back down to the car, and Amy cut loose with her story of what had been happening. Wainwright listened intently, not interrupting, and when she had finished, he said, "Perhaps you should abandon this project, at least for this year, my dear."

That wasn't the reaction she'd been looking for, and her face fell. "But Eric, it's such a good story. It's turning into a mystery now, trying to track down Le Loup. Signor Orsini won't tell me flat out that he was the man. I have to dig it out for myself. And if I can find out, I'm sure I'll have a bestseller on my hands."

His answer surprised me. "You're dealing with old wounds here, my dear, deep wounds."

"But we're talking about nearly fifty years ago." There

was a touch of the old petulance in her answer. "Most of us weren't even born then."

"Those of us who were saw a lot of ugly things happen. People lost friends, brothers, husbands, lovers." He looked every year of his age as he spoke. "Really, my dear, in the light of what happened to Pierre Armand, laying off your project would be the respectful thing to do."

"You're asking me to throw away my past year's research." She stood up, angry now, her arms folded across her chest. "There's no proof that Pierre was killed because of my work, and even if there was, it means that he died for nothing if I stop now."

It was time for some truth. "There's more to it than that," I said. "Please sit down, Amy, I have some more news, and it's even harder to take."

She stood defiantly, glaring at me. "Go ahead."

"Not until you sit down." I learned a lot from my officers' training. You don't back down on orders. I waited, looking at her until she quietly sat.

"I lied to you last night."

Eric was the first to speak. "About what?"

"When we got here last night, the dog didn't bark. I told Amy it was because he had recognized my scent. It wasn't. His throat had been cut, the same way as Pierre's."

Amy gasped. But she kept her control. "What do you think it means?"

"I know what it means because I searched Constance's apartment. She's been murdered."

Amy shrieked and sagged in her chair. Wainwright just looked at me, his mouth open in astonishment.

"And you told me everything was fine," Amy babbled. "You let me come up here and sleep as if nothing was wrong."

I said nothing. Wainwright did it for me. "It was the

right thing to do, child. I would have done the same thing. Any good officer would have done it."

So I had his approval, for whatever that was worth. He addressed his next words to me. "What did you plan to do about it today, John?"

"I figured to wait for you. It seems to me that you have a better in with the Gendarmerie than we do. You're a businessman with important contacts in this area; we're just a couple of snoops who leave death behind them as they go."

He stood up and walked over to stand behind Amy's chair, stroking her shoulders soothingly. If she noticed him, she gave no sign, and after a moment he spoke to me. "Who did it?"

"The best bet is Orsini. Or one of his heavies. I imagine he came here yesterday looking for Amy, questioned Constance, then killed her to keep her quiet." As I spoke, I remembered how tight the Armands' chauffeur had been with Orsini's man. Perhaps he had simply called and told them where Amy was. That might mean that somebody else had murdered the old lady downstairs. But I wasn't convinced. Orsini was the only guy around with a track record of murder.

"But he was so normal," Amy said. She was getting hold of herself again, and she threw in the next words, looking into my eyes almost pleadingly. "Not like last year. He was courteous, helpful. I couldn't believe it."

"What do we do next?" I put the question to Wainwright. "So far we're covered. We came home and went to sleep. Period. But everyone knows that Amy and Constance are good friends. Especially after what happened last year. People will expect us to go downstairs and say 'Hi.' We can't leave her any longer."

He took his hands from Amy's shoulders and walked over to the window. At last he turned and said softly, "I suppose the question is, what can we expect to win?"

I waited. He was thinking like a commanding officer. That was good. We needed some guidance here. It was no use simply going to the gendarmes. Someone as well schooled in nastiness as Orsini wouldn't have left any loose ends. The police wouldn't be able to pin anything on him. And if they did, he would have enough clout to squirm out through some loophole. If we were going to stay here to finish Amy's bloody book, we needed Orsini either in jail or dead.

Amy was the first to answer. A selfish answer, but I'd expected that. "I want to finish my work."

I looked at Wainwright. "Is that the object of the exercise? To let Amy finish her book?"

He looked at me, then away. We both recognized that we had a spoiled kid on our hands here, someone who wanted only what was convenient for herself. That wasn't a good enough reason to play fast and loose with the law by leaving Constance's death unreported. The only problem was that he was too caught up with Amy to be able to bring up the subject, so I did it for him, speaking directly to her. "You mean to leave Constance's body lying downstairs all summer while you flit about talking to people?"

She gasped; then her face tightened. "You have no right to talk to me like that."

"In case you hadn't noticed, this is a foreign country. They're going to be very angry if we neglect this, and I don't intend to spend time in one of their jails."

She opened her mouth to tear into me, but Wainwright held up his hand. "John's right, Amy. We can't ignore what's happened. We have to find some way to help the police. If we do that, they'll be better disposed to let you continue your work."

She threw her hands in the air. "What can we do? The place was crawling with gendarmes yesterday when Pierre was killed, but they've done nothing."

"They've done what they can. The investigation is still going on. You can't expect them to solve a murder in twenty minutes." I was beginning to hate myself for taking this tack. I'd seen Constance. I was personally angry enough to find the guy who'd done it and tear his head off, but here I was the voice of sweet reason.

Wainwright turned and looked out of the window again. It didn't seem as if he was any better able to find an answer than I was. It was time to give him more facts. "Eric. If you wouldn't mind. Can I speak to you in private, please?"

Amy stood up angrily. "Oh, that's fine. The men will get together and talk sense and then put their tails between their legs and run away where it's safe. That's great!" She shoved her chair under the table, so violently that it tipped over. But she didn't pause to right it. She stormed off upstairs.

Wainwright watched her go, looking as if he wanted to follow her and tell her everything was going to be all right. When he didn't turn back to me, I said, "Okay. Let's sit down and discuss this thing calmly. I've got some information that may be useful."

Now he turned his back on the stairs and walked with me to the end of the sitting room, where he sat down in an armchair. I sat on the couch that had been my bed. "There are things going on that have nothing to do with Amy," I said.

"Such as?" I had his attention now.

"Such as pressure on the Armands from Orsini. He's

trying to push them out of business and take over. Hélène told me that much."

He allowed himself the ghost of a smile. "And you always believe anything a beautiful woman tells you?"

"She asked me to kill Orsini. And then their chauffeur tried to kill her, and finally, two thugs from out of town tried to abduct her last night as Amy and I were trying to leave the place. I stopped them. I figured they were after Amy, but Hélène wanted me to kill them, to shove their car over a cliff somewhere."

His smile vanished. "This is very serious."

"It's why we're having this talk. So far as I can make out, Amy has fallen into the middle of some kind of squabble between Armand and Orsini. The gendarmes are blaming her because that's the way the police mind works, but the truth is, there's a war going on here."

He sat for a long moment, then said, "But how would that cause the death of the old woman downstairs?"

"Beats the hell out of me. I've told you my guess, that Orsini came here looking for Amy."

"And yet when he came to visit her, he was courteous. She told me that herself." Wainwright had lost his objectivity. A soldier or a cop would have wondered about Orsini's good behavior. It meant either that there had been something phony about Amy's story of the previous year's encounter or that the guy was planning something sneaky. But Wainwright didn't seem able to analyze what he'd heard. He accepted it as gospel and never wondered about it, like a novice in Holy Orders.

I pushed the conversation ahead. "What it boils down to is this. What do we gain by not going to the police?"

Wainwright rubbed his eyebrow with his forefinger. It's a thing only old men or actors ever do. But it seemed to help his thinking. "Nothing," he said at last. It was the sensible answer, but he muddied it up immediately. "But it means that Amy loses her chance to work, and that costs her a year of research."

I was about to tell him that not calling the police could cost her a year or two of her freedom, but I didn't have the chance. From up on the hill behind the house came the crisp, echoing report of a rifle shot.

I dropped to my knees and craned up slightly to peek out of the window. Chrétien was lying beside the car, blood seeping out of a hole in his shirtfront. I pulled back my head, and in the next instant there was a vicious whine, chased by the sound of the rifle shot as a second bullet ricocheted off the stone sill, inches from my face.

CHAPTER

12

BEHIND ME I heard Wainwright gasp, and I turned to him. "Your driver's hit. Could be dead. It looks bad."

"Good God." He was grim but not panicky; that was good news. His war had been a long time ago, but he hadn't lost the old reflexes. I pulled out the revolver. "Get up to Amy's room. Take this with you and keep them out if they come for her."

"Right. What are you going to do?"

"Constance has a phone downstairs. I'm going to call the police." I set the gun down on the floor and ducked away below the level of the window, toward the back door of the apartment.

He took the gun, then dropped flat to squirm past the window and make for the stairs. Amy's face appeared at the door of her room. "Stay in there, I'm coming up," he said, and ran up the stairs at surprising speed for a man of his age, shoving her back through the doorway. They would be safe if they stayed put. Even the inside walls of the house were made of thick stone. Unless the guy on the hill had a heavier-caliber weapon than the one he'd used on Chrétien, his bullets wouldn't break through to them.

And if they stayed low, in the corner, he would have no chance of hitting them with a bullet through the roof.

I eased the front door open. Nobody fired. If there was only one man out there, I was safe. The roof of the drive shed where the cars were kept was too low for my movements to be seen from the hill. I would be under cover until I got to ground level.

I didn't use the steps. Instead, I crouched low on the flat area outside the door and dropped the six feet to the ground, rolling in behind my car. Glancing up, I checked that I was still out of sight, unless the man had come down the hill almost level with me, so I stood up to check the window in the wall. It was closed, and I rolled again, behind Constance's car now, to reach her back door.

It was an ancient thing of crude planks painted gray. The lock had been put in a hundred years ago; it took a big old key that might have gotten me into the Bastille. I checked that it was locked and then straightened and slammed it with my foot. The lock held, but the shock was too much for the tired old timbers, and the middle of the door caved in. I hit it again, and it gave completely, allowing me to force it once more with my shoulder and split it in two.

I ducked inside as a bullet smashed through the tiles on the roof behind me, zinging angrily around the confined space.

If anybody had been waiting, they would have been in the corridor, aiming at me as I came through the door, so I flattened myself against the far wall, covering the room with my pistol. Nothing moved. I'd seen the telephone in her living room, so I headed that way, keeping below the level of the back window. There was still a chance that another man was waiting in the living room. I knew first-hand how easy it was to break in, or there could be a second sniper, out in the oak trees in front of the house, waiting for me to come into view as I went for the phone.

I crouched at the doorway, listening. Nothing moved in the room. All I could hear was the faint buzzing of the first flies to discover Constance's body. After a pause I stepped into the room and rolled behind the couch, then knelt up to cover the area with my gun. The place was empty except for Constance, and she didn't count anymore, thanks to Orsini. The telephone sat on a coffee table next to her favorite chair. I grabbed the whole unit and ducked back behind the couch, scanning the orchard as I moved, checking for movement or the glint of a weapon.

Nothing moved outside, and I lifted the receiver and waited for the dial tone. But there was none. A glance told me that the wall connection had been torn out of the wall. I swore automatically, then started thinking. Perhaps there was only one man, on the hill behind us. From there he could cover any attempt to get away, once our car reached the driveway. But that would call for some fancy shooting on his part, and some luck. No, they probably had a second man outside, down in the bushes, waiting for us. He could drop the driver with one shot and kill or abduct the survivors with no trouble.

That seemed the best placement for limited numbers, but it didn't mean there was no one outside the French windows at my level. I paused and weighed the signs again. If they had a sniper out there, he would have taken a shot at me as I came in. All things considered, it was worth trying to get out.

I'd noticed a big old sun hat on a peg in the kitchen, and I doubled back out there and grabbed it, then came back to the big room and rolled across to the wall beside the French window. There was a blue Chinese vase on a low table next to me, and I hung the hat on it and then sneaked the hat sideways until it showed at the corner of the window, moving it as carefully as if my head were inside. From the oak trees it would have looked like a living target, and a sniper would have snapped off a shot. But none came.

It meant either there was nobody out there or that he was smarter than me. There's a lot of that going around, but I still had to try. The motto of my old unit is Who Dares, Wins, and I subscribe to it as one of the all-time truths. This was the chance to test the theory. I stood up and opened the French window, diving through it in a long roll, then crouching and diving the other way as I made for the east side of the house. There was a banked-up flower bed there, and I lay behind it for half a minute, sheltered from the orchard side by its height and from the hill by the bulk of the house itself.

I still had the old hat in my left hand, and I used it again as a target, holding it out by the brim, a few inches past the side of the house. From the way Chrétien's body had been lying, I figured I was screened from the rifleman until I got to the north corner of the house, close to the shed and back door where I'd entered Constance's quarters. If my hat trick was the litmus test, I was right. No shots came.

Staying low, I ducked around the corner of the house, past the dead dog, which was getting high and attracting most of the flies in the region. I ran to the corner, staying behind it, still out of sight of the hill, and looked around for a stick. There was an old olive tree near the wall, and I took out my knife and snicked off a low branch, taking care not to shake the top of the tree, which could be seen from the hill. Now came the daring bit.

I stuck the sharp end of the branch into the fabric of the hat and crept back to the corner. There I paused a moment to check behind me. Nobody there. Good. I lay down behind the corner, right hand holding my pistol, thinking. If the guy with the rifle was good, I would only have one chance at this. It was time to take the risk. Inch at a time, I eased my head around the corner until I was able to see up the hill out of my right eye. Then I raised the branch behind me and tilted it until the hat was showing around the corner. Within a second a rifle shot blazed off the wall, missing the hat but uncomfortably close to me. I pulled the hat back, dropping it behind me against the wall. I still had not seen the rifleman, but the angle of the shot narrowed my search area, and I saw the only place it could have come from. It was a bush, lower on the slope than he had been when he first fired.

The knowledge that he was moving cut down my options. There was no time to double around the house and take him from the other side. He might be gone before I reached it, already inside the house, where it would be harder to winkle him out. This was showdown time.

I dived and rolled to my right, coming up on one knee and putting three quick shots into the bush, combing it left to right. It worked. I heard a scream and a clatter and saw the rifle tumble away down the slope. I'd hit him.

There was no way of knowing how badly he was hit or whether he had a second weapon, so I played it smart, diving and rolling again, coming up close enough to the woodpile to huddle down and be out of sight of the bush. I crouched there a long moment, checking all around me and listening hard. The major sound was the sawing of the cicadas basking in the heat, but under it I made out the angry whimper of the wounded man. He wasn't faking it; he was hurt.

I did the dumb, necessary thing. I left the shelter of the woodpile and charged up the hill, not directly at him but on the easiest path, heading to a spot thirty feet to his left and ten feet above the bush. I saw him almost at once, sprawled back but clenching both hands around the wound in his thigh. If he had a second gun, he wasn't thinking of using it right then. He was wishing he'd gone straight when he was a kid. I took the final few paces and stuck my pistol in his face. All the French I know had flown from my mind, and I snarled at him in English, counting on the gun to do the translating for me. "Put your hands up."

He looked at me helplessly, so I tapped his hands with the muzzle of my Walther. It was still warm from the shots, and he understood, putting both his hands on his head and lying back helplessly. I patted him down, finding no gun but taking a switchblade and a handful of rifle shells from his pants pockets. "Roll over," I commanded, making a circling motion with the muzzle. He babbled something but did as I said, half-screaming as he put pressure on his wounded leg. He had nothing else on him, and I left him there, stuffing the shells into my jacket pocket and grabbing up the rifle as I ran past it down the hill.

It was steeper than is comfortable, and I ended up having to run almost to the drive shed before I could break speed. My adrenaline was pumping as if I were on street patrol under sniper fire in Belfast, and I checked the drive shed for other enemies before taking the stone steps three at a time and reaching the apartment.

"It's okay. I've stopped him," I said. "You can come down."

Wainwright came out first, dangling the pistol from his right hand. He asked the practical question. "Is he dead?"

"No. He's hit in the thigh. I was firing blind."

"Good show," he said enthusiastically. He turned and called, "Come on Amy, it's all right, John has wounded the man."

He came down the stairs and took the rifle from me. "A Kalishnikov," he said wonderingly.

"No, it's the Israeli copy, a Galil." I took out the shells I'd found in the prisoner's pocket and reloaded the magazine. Amy watched me without speaking. She was very pale.

"You've used one of these?" Wainwright asked.

"I know how to. We trained on everybody's weapons in the SAS."

"Good." He nodded briskly. "What do you suggest now?"

"The phone's out. We can't call the police, but we can get information out of Alphonse there, on the hill."

"Is he alone?"

"I'm not sure. If I'd been running things, I'd have put a second man in the driveway somewhere to stop us if we made a dash for it."

"Then we can't go for a phone," he said.

"I'll do it. I'll take the rifle and head across country to the gas station."

Wainwright frowned at me. "Is that wise? Wouldn't it be better to neutralize the man on the drive?"

"Is that necessary? He'll probably run when the gendarmes come down the driveway; he's not counting on being taken from the rear."

"What if he attacks when you're away?" His voice was calm, but the question surprised me. The odds were against the guy's making a move. If he was on the drive somewhere, he probably wouldn't have heard the yell out of his partner. He'd be waiting down there, snug as a bug behind his bank until his buddy came down for him, grinning with the news that the mission was completed.

"I think we should mop up," Wainwright said firmly. "Can you manage it?"

"I can try. Wait here and I'll bring the other guy in."

I took a moment to slip the magazine out of the rifle, eject the last round, and check that the barrel was clear. I didn't want to blow my hand off with a back blast from a plugged muzzle.

It was clean, so I reloaded and cocked the weapon. "Stay low," I ordered, and went back out to retrieve my man.

There was no one else around, and the guy was anxious to do as he was told, so I hooked his arm over my shoulder and steered him down the slope to the house, listening to his sobs of pain close to my ear as he took part of his weight on his wounded leg.

Amy had put the kettle on and was tearing up a clean sheet. "Put him on the couch," she said briskly. I set him down there and cut his pant leg away above the wound.

"Right. Eric, keep your eyes open and the gun handy," I said, and went back out, checking carefully, then heading to the east side of the house and making my way ahead to the far side of the oak orchard. I'd already worked out the best place for an ambush, down where the driveway was the ruttiest and a car would have to creep. There was a steep bank there with an ancient willow tree growing out of it, ideal cover, on the far side of the drive from the house. It figured to be the spot where trouble would come from, so I kept moving out until I was clear of the whole area, then slipped across the lane back where it doubled around from the old coach road toward the last bend in front of the house.

My clothes are chosen carefully in case I ever have to carry out this kind of maneuver on an assignment. I was wearing tan slacks and a light brown jacket, not camouflage exactly but neutral enough to blend in here among the deep shadows of the trees down the drive. Moving as carefully as if I were on jungle patrol, I eased through the undergrowth along the tiny stream that tinkled down beside the driveway. I made no sound.

It took almost half an hour to cover a hundred yards and reach a point twenty paces south of the big willow. There I paused, crouching and checking all around me for any movement. Nothing was stirring, but my first deep breath told me I was right. The bloody amateur was smoking.

In a few seconds more I saw him, lying at the side of the tree, holding a long-barreled shotgun, puffing away happily on his cigarette.

Infinitely slowly, I inched up behind him and then clubbed him between the shoulder blades with the butt of the rifle. He gasped and collapsed forward, clutching at his gun. I reversed the rifle and tapped him on the head with the muzzle. *"En haute les mains."* My Gallic version of hands up.

He let go of the gun and pushed his hands up, craning around to see who had done this to him. I nudged his head again with the muzzle, doing it hard enough to hurt so he knew I wasn't kidding.

"Combien des autres avec toi?" How many others with you?

"*Seulement un.*" If he wasn't lying, it meant we'd won.

"*Si n'est pas vrai, je te fusille.*" I said grimly. If that's not true, I'll shoot you. My French would have earned a C minus in school, but here it was aces. He nodded and babbled something.

"*Marche,*" I commanded, and he scrambled up, keeping his hands high. Out of sheer malice I paused long enough to stab the muzzle of the shotgun deep into the soft earth by the tree roots, then wipe it off so the gun looked normal but was a death trap for the unwary. I left it there and followed him, checking all around for other movement. There was none, and I made him double up the driveway until he was ready to collapse. Really, smoking is the pits for fitness.

I ran him around the corner of the house toward the drive shed and the door of the apartment. The speed saved my life. As I came to the corner of the shed, a man stepped out from behind the woodpile and blazed off a pistol shot at me. I cut him down with a squirt from the Galil. And then I heard Wainwright's voice, hoarse and frightened. "Drop the gun, John, or they'll kill Amy."

If this had been a battle against rational enemies, I would have done it, trusting to the Geneva convention to protect us all. But I'd seen what these men did to prisoners, so I did the logical thing. I reversed the rifle and slammed my prisoner in the back of the neck, taking him out of the equation.

Wainwright shouted, "What are you doing? He'll kill her."

"Tell him I don't believe it," I said evenly. "If he harms her, I'll blow his balls off."

There was a confusion of voices speaking French, then

a half scream from Amy. "John! For God's sake. He's got a gun."

"Tell him to bring you outside." I was assessing my choices and checking all around to see there was nobody else in view. It was clear. Whoever had taken them was inside with them.

"He can't walk. You wounded him." She screamed.

"Then tell him I don't believe him. Have him bring you to the window."

I backed away from the man I'd dropped until I was squarely in front of the window from which I'd seen Chrétien's body. And I waited through another angry torrent of French until finally Amy's face appeared at the window. And then at last I saw the sneering face of the man from the hill.

He had a pistol against her cheek. It looked like the Colt I'd given Wainwright. And the damn fool hadn't even cocked it. It would take him a double pressure to cock and fire. I didn't pause but raised the rifle and snapped off a single shot, right through his open mouth. It's the shot they teach American SWAT teams, severing the spinal cord so there is no reflexive jerk on the trigger as he dies.

His body flew back out of my sight and blood spurted out, onto Amy, making her scream with horror, then lean through the window and retch helplessly. I paused long enough to check that my prisoner was still out of it, then ran into the drive shed and up the steps to the apartment.

Amy was still at the window, but the man I'd shot was sprawled back across the back of a couch, the back of his head smashed. Wainwright was crouching beside him, his own face chalk white.

"Good God. What have you done?" He almost screamed it.

"Saved all our lives, I'd imagine," I said. "How did this happen?"

Before he could answer, Amy turned from the window and screeched at me. "His blood is all over me!"

"He can't hurt you now," I said.

"He wasn't going to hurt me," she said, sobbing. "He promised that. He promised."

I ignored her. If I'd surrendered, both he and his buddy would have been tearing her clothes off by now, making sure Wainwright and I saw what happened. And afterward they would have killed all three of us, taking their own sweet time, getting creative with their knives. "How did this happen?" I repeated.

Wainwright spoke at last, standing up painfully, bracing his right hand on his knee.

"We were in here, dressing this man's wound. And then the guy outside came in with that gun. He made me give the pistol to the prisoner; then he went outside to wait for you."

"That second bastard told me there weren't any more," I said angrily. I was shaky myself now, coming down from the combat high, realizing how much explaining I'd have to do to a squad of bored French policemen who hadn't been here to see what happened. For a moment I was almost glad that Contance had been murdered. That was a motive at least for what I'd had to do.

Wainwright didn't help. He stood looking at me as if I were a leper. "You're a cold man," he said.

"Get some coffee going," I told him. "You should be able to handle that."

He disgusted me. I'd left him a simple job to do. If he'd

done it instead of helping Amy play Florence Nightingale, the guy on the couch would still be alive—in lots of trouble but at least able to look forward to a fair trial. Now he was gone and with him part of my chance to clear things up with the gendarmes.

Amy passed me, running to the bathroom. The door slammed, and I heard her retching again, then the sound of running water. Wainwright slowly went to the kitchen and filled the coffeepot. By the time he had finished, Amy came out of the bathroom, her face cleaned up and blood sponged away from her T-shirt so that the stains hardly showed.

She stood at the door, looking at me down the length of the room. I saw her face set, and slowly she walked toward where I stood, the Galil cradled in my right elbow. I wondered if she was going to do something theatrical like slapping my face, but she surprised me. "I'm very sorry for what I said, John. You did what was right."

"My job." I nodded.

"Thank you. You saved all our lives," she said, and she craned up on tiptoe to kiss me on the lips. It was more stunning than a slap would have been, and I didn't know how to respond. But I didn't have to. Faintly, from the roadway, then closer as they turned down the old coach road to the farm, came the sound of police sirens. Somebody had finally heard the shooting and called the gendarmes.

CHAPTER

13

FORTUNATELY for me, Labrosse was in the lead car. Any other gendarme finding Frenchmen with my bullets in them would have locked me up first, taken a statement second. But Labrosse was a pro. He took me aside and listened to my story without interrupting. He got a little tight-lipped when I told him I'd found Constance's body the night before and made the decision to wait for morning before reporting it, but he said nothing until I'd finished.

Then he had two of his men carry the survivor into the apartment and set Amy to work on reviving him. I'd put the guy to sleep pretty deeply, but as soon as he opened his eyes, Labrosse started asking questions.

Wainwright had surrendered the Colt, and I gave up the Galil, and we sat on the couch waiting for Labrosse to get around to us. Wainwright was listening intently as the injured man talked. I couldn't follow the conversation— it was too fast and idiomatic for me—but I could tell from a little nod that Wainwright gave that he felt justified in whatever he'd been thinking. However, it was Labrosse who spoke to me first.

"This man says he was out hunting rabbits when you attacked him."

"How big do your rabbits grow that he needed double O buckshot?"

Labrosse's face creased in a microscopic grin. "Not the usual load." He turned back to the man, jabbing a finger into his face.

The man was recovered enough by now to realize the jam he was in, and he changed his tune. He sang it for five full minutes. At last Labrosse turned to me again. "Now he remembers better," he said.

"Does he remember who sent him?"

"A gentleman from Marseilles. No name, unfortunately, but there is time for him to think more."

"If it was Marseilles, then it had to be Orsini."

Labrosse clicked his tongue impatiently. *"Venez!"* he commanded, then translated for me, although I had understood. "Come." He led the way downstairs and outside to the flat area behind the house, where the bodies of Chrétien and the second man I'd shot were still lying, covered now with sheets from the apartment's linen closet.

"I have heard that Orsini visited Miss Roger yesterday."

"He did. And he was charming to her. No hint of this kind of badness. I find it hard to understand what's happening, Captain."

"Me also." He paced slowly, looking up the hill to the bush, where I had wounded the first man. Watching him work was like watching a hunting dog. Nothing about him was idle. Every glance seemed to have a purpose; I wondered if he ever relaxed, ever forgot what he did for a living.

"I have heard many things since we spoke yesterday," he said. "For example, I have heard that two injured men were found in a Mercedes with no keys not twenty kilometers from here. One of them says that a blond English-man attacked them."

I waited for the other shoe to drop. He had some-thing a little delicate in his head; otherwise, he would simply have arrested me. Hell, I'd caused enough com-motion that sticking me inside would have earned him stars on his work. The charges would probably have been dropped later, but right now I'd look good on ice. I stood there, waiting for him to make the running. Finally, he went on, speaking slowly, as if he were still working things out.

"I also had a talk to Grégoire, the manager for M'sieur Armand. He tells me that two men came to the house last night and that an Englishman staying with the family hit them both on the head."

"These are violent times, Captain."

"Indeed. One is reminded of Algeria." He was musing now, almost as if I weren't there. "The only difference is that I have men now who have never fought a war. They have taken training, as I have, but they are police, not true soldiers."

He paused a moment, and I stood waiting, listening to the cicadas sawing away, waiting for him to make his point. At last he said, "If this blond Englishman would work for me, I would find out many things. I would find, for ex-ample, the name of the man who employs other men to kill an old woman."

"Perhaps the Englishman would not want to do such a thing." Two can play at the third-person game. It was just a hair less worrying than talking turkey. But he soon put an end to that feeling.

"Then I would have to look for him and put him in my

cells," he said. "These men he hit have told me how he looks; he would not be hard to find."

So there it was. Good news and bad news. The good news was I could stay out of jail. The bad news was that I had to buy my freedom by wrestling an alligator.

"I believe I know this man, Captain. He could be convinced if I spoke to him. What would you want him to do?"

"I would want him to take Orsini somewhere and talk to him, without lawyers and newspapers and photographs and all the things that would prevent a gendarme from finding the truth."

Well, now I knew which alligator I would be wrestling; that was a start. But I didn't roll over and play dead. "This man does not speak French well enough to talk to Orsini."

"That is of no importance. A French speaker will go also."

A French speaker—not a Frenchman. I wondered who he had in mind. "What will happen to Miss Roger while I am away talking to my friend?"

"She will be in no danger while your friend talks to Orsini, and she will be permitted to continue her work."

"In that case, I will talk to this man. But first you must tell me where Orsini is so I can brief him."

"Good." He dropped his cigarette and stepped on it. And for the next few minutes he filled me in. Orsini was staying at a château near Avignon. Labrosse figured he was in the region to deal with the people who were doing his work here, the enforcers and loan sharks. He did not customarily carry weapons himself, but he would have at least one armed bodyguard, and it was likely that the other men with him would be carrying. When captured, he should be blindfolded and brought to the Armands' house, where he would be interrogated.

The choice of venue surprised me. I had guessed the day before that there was no love lost between Armand and Orsini, but it seemed like a security risk to take an illegal prisoner to a spot where there were so many potential witnesses. But I didn't question it. Instead, I asked who was to go with this friend of mine.

"I believe that M'sieur Wainwright will volunteer," Labrosse said. "Let us go and tell them the plan."

We went back in, and Labrosse did the talking in machine-gun bursts of French that made Wainwright and Amy look at one another in consternation.

They both had things to say, but Labrosse talked them down, using management skills, wearing a tight little smile to indicate that this was all friendly and relaxed, that it was just a suggestion. But his tone was a reminder not to forget who was doing the suggesting.

When Labrosse finished, Wainwright looked at me. "All right, then, old chap, let's go and find this friend of yours."

Amy broke in immediately. "This is ridiculous, Eric. You shouldn't be doing this. Neither should John. It's dangerous."

"It's a preemptive strike," I said. "Believe me, this is less dangerous than hanging around waiting for Orsini to send someone else."

Amy burst into tears and clung to Wainwright, but he disengaged her hands and patted her gently on the shoulder. "Don't worry, my dear. John is very good at this kind of thing. We'll be fine."

"We'll be finer if you can take the Colt you had this morning," I suggested. Labrosse looked at me without speaking, then picked up the Colt from the table, where he had set it down, broke it open for safety, and handed it to Wainwright without a word. The old man checked the load and snapped it shut, shoving it into his jacket pocket.

"Right," he said. "Let's get cracking, shall we?" Get cracking! I could see he was still mentally fighting World War II.

We left them and went down to my car. I drove, with Wainwright sitting up straight in his seat, looking all around as if we were on patrol in enemy country. When we got to the road, he asked, "Where are we going?"

"To Avignon—near there, anyway. There's a château where Orsini stays. The object of the exercise is to bring him out—unharmed, if possible—and transport him to the Armands', where he's to be blindfolded and questioned. I thought Labrosse explained that."

"He did," Wainwright said. "But this is ridiculous. If we get caught, it means twenty years in prison. I'd never get out alive."

"Then why didn't you say no to Labrosse?"

"He said only that I was to go with this mythical friend of yours and talk to Orsini. He wants to know what's going on."

"Don't tell me you bought a line of crap like that." I glanced at him in dismay. Why was he lying to me? I had no doubt that Labrosse had made it perfectly clear. I wondered if he was going to chicken out on me now that Amy wasn't around to watch him playing hero. But he was all the help I had, and I needed a plan. "Any suggestions on how we can get in without getting searched?"

The question helped Wainwright get his head together. He sat back in his seat, frowning gently. At last he said,

"The best thing might be to bring a gift of some kind. That might put them off guard."

"What kind of gift?" My mind was jumping ahead. Perhaps we could set ourselves up a Trojan horse.

"A really excellent wine is always welcome," he said at last. "Yes, that would be it." He glanced around at the road with new interest. "Pity we're here, the Côtes du Rhône aren't impressive. We need a Burgundy."

I cut through the oenophilia. "Can we pick up something passable anywhere around here?"

He frowned and looked as if he were going to argue, so I cut in again. "We're not catering a royal wedding, we're looking for a Trojan horse. In fact, for the thing I've got in mind, cognac would be better."

"Cognac? Are you planning to drink him under the table?"

"Cognac," I repeated. "Let's do it my way."

Cognac proved more of a problem than wine. We couldn't just drive into a *cave* and pick the best of their stock. Down this far south the only cognac to be had is from the supermarket or the bars. We ended up in the big *supermarché* in Vaison, buying a case of reasonable stuff. It wasn't a *grande marque*, at least nothing I'd heard of, but Wainwright was satisfied.

I put the car in gear and headed out onto the street. "So far, so good. Next stop is somewhere they sell fireworks."

"Fireworks." Wainwright looked at me, narrowing his eyes, then laughed suddenly. "I say. What a marvelous idea."

"The country should be full of the things. Next week is the bicentennial of Bastille Day. Someone ought to be able to spare us some firepower."

In fact, it wasn't as easy as that, but Wainwright was

able to talk some hardware storekeeper into parting with a few rockets. We went to a different store to buy the rest of the things I needed. They included a stout plastic jar, some batteries, wire, a burglar-alarm device, a roll of friction tape, and a couple of cheap disposable cigarette lighters.

We pulled off the road about ten kilometers from Orsini's place, and I worked for half an hour, sweating like a bull in the heat of the car. First I broke the fireworks in half and stuffed them into the plastic jar. Then I taped down the control on one of the cigarette lighters so it leaked butane nonstop. I dropped it into the jar, then the intact one. I'd already set up the electrical contacts, and now I laid them inside the jar and screwed the top on, sealing the jar with electrical tape so that some oxygen would remain inside, enough to support the combustion when the spark flew. Finally, I set up the triggering device so it would operate when the top of the case of cognac was opened. The top looked untouched, as if it had never been tampered with. I'd done all my insertions from the bottom.

Wainwright had been out of the car, at my suggestion, playing it safe in case anything went wrong.

"Right," I told him, making a typical British military joke, using the proper nomenclature for description of equipment. "Traps, booby, one, hoodlums for the entrapment of."

"Are you sure it will detonate?" His war was almost fifty years in the past. He knew that equipment had changed since then, but he didn't trust it.

"Yes." I didn't expand on it, just stepped out of the car for a moment to allow the sweat to dry on my back. I caught a whiff of myself and realized I needed a shower. Later. I had a lot more sweat to work up first.

Wainwright stood looking at me across the roof of the car. "Were you an explosives man in the army?"

"No. We had an expert on our team. I was the weapons man. Particularly pistol." It's not gentlemanly to talk up your achievements, but if asked nicely, I would have been glad of the chance to tell him that my nickname had been Cowboy. Partly because I was the only North American on the team but mostly because I generally hit what I aim at.

Wainwright was nostalgic for his own salad days. "It was more or less the same in my day. Each man had a specific task, but any one of us could fill in for any other."

"What was your speciality?"

"Languages and unarmed combat," he said, and grinned. "Seems silly now, with all my joints starting to creak, but I used to be very good."

"How stiff are your joints?" I dropped down into the seat and started the motor, then turned and set the booby-trapped case carefully on the backseat. Wainwright got in and answered my question.

"Given the element of surprise, I could still take out a man at close quarters. Probably permanently."

I knew what that meant. He had been trained on the breakneck holds. Left arm around a victim's neck, right hand shoving, using the left elbow as the fulcrum, unhinging the victim's neck neatly. A two-second murder. Great while Hitler was the captain of the opposing team, but if we did that here, Labrosse would start getting annoyed.

"Better cool it. We're up to quota on dead Frenchmen."

He snorted with amusement, and we drove on to the château where Orsini was staying. It was unexceptional, a two-hundred-year-old country mansion with a fifty-meter driveway leading to it from the road.

"Here goes," I said, and turned into the drive and headed for the house, moving fast enough to be a tough target but not so fast as to look guilty. I could see Orsini's car standing outside the front door, and I recognized the chauffeur. He was my sparring partner from the day before. He looked up at our car as I drove in, and I saw his hand go around to the back of his belt. Then the other front door of the car opened, and a second man slipped out, staying low behind the car. There was a third man in the back, sitting up curiously in the seat. Orsini!

"Bingo," I said. "Hold on to your hat." I wheeled up the wrong way around the circular drive in front of the house, coming up nose on to Orsini's car and a few feet to the left side. The chauffeur took a step back as I approached, but I slammed my door open, catching him broadside. He flew back against his car, and I jammed my brakes on and rolled out of the front seat before the guy behind the car had chance to draw a bead on me. I pulled my weapon as I rolled, coming up on the far side of Orsini's car, level with the bodyguard. He had his gun in his hand, but he was way out of sequence with the speed of events, craning up over his own car, expecting me to be standing up beside my door, as if we'd called socially. I had the drop on him, and he knew it. I guess my reputation had been talked up downstairs in the Orsini ménage. He looked at me cunningly but lowered his gun.

"Drop it," I told him. He probably didn't speak English, but he looked at me for a long moment, then let the gun fall. I walked over and kicked it away. *"A bas,"* I said, and gestured to the ground. The man sat but I motioned impatiently with the gun and he rolled over and lay facedown. *"Restez là,"* I told him. Stay there. I wanted to make sure the other man was disarmed, for I'd learned to mistrust Wainwright's abilities.

I stepped to where I could see both sides of the car at once, covering both my guy and the chauffeur. He didn't seem much of a threat. He was lying on his back with his feet drawn up, clutching his gut where the door had winded him. Wainwright was standing over him, his gun drawn.

"Cover him and frisk him carefully. He's carrying," I ordered.

Wainwright crouched and spoke to the man sharply in French, and the guy groaned and rolled over painfully. Wainwright patted him down. He drew a gun from a belt holster and held it up triumphantly. I patted him on the shoulder and went back to the bodyguard. He was on his hands and knees now, but he subsided when he saw me again, and I frisked him, taking a knife from his left sock. All the time I was working I stayed alert, waiting for re-inforcements to show up from the door of the house, but it stayed closed, and Orsini stayed where he was, in the backseat, sitting impassively. For all the emotion he was showing, he might have been waiting for a green light.

The bodyguard was wearing slip-on shoes, so there were no laces I could use to tie his thumbs together. "Bring the electrical tape from the car," I called, and Wainwright brought it to me. I quickly wrapped the guy's wrists. It wasn't ideal. He would be free in twenty minutes, but with luck we would be long gone by then.

"Get Orsini out and stand him beside our car," I told Wainwright. "Look menacing or he won't buy it."

"Right." He tapped on Orsini's window with his gun, and Orsini looked at him, not stirring. I ignored them both and went and taped the chauffeur's wrists. I could hear

Wainwright talking in French, but there was no sound of a door opening.

"What's going on?" I asked when the second man was secure.

"He says he won't get out. The glass is bulletproof."

"Ask him if it's fireproof," I instructed. "Tell him he's got ten seconds to get out or I stuff a rag in the gas tank and strike a match."

Wainwright spoke rapidly, and I saw a flicker in Orsini's eyes. Not fear—he was too much of a man for that—but respect for an idea as ruthless as something he might have come up with. He held both hands palms up in a gesture of acceptance, I wouldn't have called it surrender; he was too proud for that. Then he opened the door, and I grabbed him and pushed him up against the car, searching him quickly for a weapon. He was clean, and I stuck my gun back in its holster and taped his hands together behind his back. Then I pulled the handkerchief from his top pocket and laid it over his eyes, taping it in place with enough strips to mask his vision completely.

Wainwright earned his keep. He was acting like a soldier, keeping his eyes open, checking the two men on the ground and the house for any sign of interference. He had his gun in his hand the whole time, ready for use. The guy who got the drop on him at the farm earlier in the day had given him a refresher course in all the soldierly skills he had learned in the Guards fifty years earlier.

When I had Orsini blindfolded properly, I paused to stick my knife into both back tires of the Mercedes; then we steered Orsini into the backseat of my car and drove out.

"Somebody indoors may have seen us and called the cops," I said. "I'm going to turn off this road and take back ways."

"I doubt if anyone in this man's employ would call the police," Wainwright said. "But they may have called in reinforcements, other men from somewhere else. It's wise to take evasive action."

There is not a big choice of roads in the area, but I managed to loop around enough different ways that there was no logic to our track, no obvious direction established. If anyone should try to backtrack us, they would go crazy trying to pick a destination. The maneuvering took me an hour or so, and it was after twelve before we came close to the Armand house.

"Soon be there," Wainwright said.

"I'm not anxious to wheel up to the front door like this," I said. Now that we had done what Labrosse had asked for, I was starting to wonder why he had needed me at all. The French police have wider powers than their equivalents in our country. He could have pulled Orsini in and talked to him through normal channels. His little speech about newspapers and lawyers was starting to sound phony now that I'd broken the law in his behalf.

"What's the problem?" Wainwright asked. "You didn't have any reservations earlier on, when we were picking this chap up."

"Labrosse blackmailed me," I argued. "When he said what he wanted, I was too concerned about what I'd already done to argue with him. Now I've had time to think."

"There's nothing to worry about." Wainwright shook his head firmly. "You've got me—and Amy, for that matter—as witnesses. We'll testify that you were coerced into doing this."

The gates of the Armand château were looming ahead of us. I flicked on the turn signals and pulled into the driveway. "Let's just hope you're right," I said.

"Count on it, old boy," Wainwright said, but he seemed tense.

I crunched the car slowly up the driveway, wondering what was different about the place. And then I realized there were no children playing around the front of the house. Armand must have shipped the family out so they wouldn't witness Orsini's arrival.

Labrosse was standing on the patio. He stooped to see into the car, then signaled to me to keep on going, around to the stables. I nodded and drove on. I didn't speak. Orsini did not need to know where he was. If I made any comments, he might realize where he had been taken, and that could mean reprisals later.

I drove into the stable yard and saw Armand standing at the mouth of one of the double garages. It was empty, and he beckoned me over, indicating that I should pull in to the right. I did as he wanted, and he pressed a button that rolled the garage door down behind us.

I turned off the ignition and got out of the car warily. My personal alarm system was on red alert. It seemed that Labrosse and Armand were planning for Orsini to make a lot of noise. That was something for me to size up as it happened. Interrogations aren't usually social occasions, but I wouldn't sit still for torture no matter what Orsini was supposed to have done.

I looked at Armand closely. He was standing beside the door, arms folded, face set. He was wearing a gray suit, a city suit, not like the more countrified clothes he had worn the day before. He looked formal, as if he had business to attend to. And in the lapel he sported a tiny insignia. I glanced at it, as I do at anybody's self-advertisement. This one startled me. It was the double-bladed cross of Lorraine, the symbol of the French Resistance. From what he'd said,

I had thought he was a prisoner throughout the war. Apparently not.

Wainwright got out of the car more slowly and spoke to Armand. I didn't understand what he said, but I recognized that he used the familiar pronoun *tu*. That's a privilege you don't get from doing business with another man's company. It's either a sign of contempt, as it had been when I used it on the man I'd captured earlier, or it's a privilege, denoting familiarity, either family or the kind of association you earn by serving together in the same military unit.

"What happens now?" I asked Wainwright.

"We wait for Captain Labrosse," he said. "Would you be so kind as to get Mr. Orsini out of the car, please."

I nodded and opened the back door of the car. Orsini turned his head toward me behind its blind black mask. I was reminded of a falcon under its hood, all the hunting and killing skills on hold, until the eyes were uncovered.

Wainwright and Armand were talking, standing close together, clattering at one another in rapid, angry-sounding French. And suddenly I understood what was happening. This was not a criminal investigation of Orsini. This was to be an inquiry, a trial even, for crimes committed forty-five years ago, when Armand and Wainwright and Labrosse's father had been young men, young Resistance fighters. The three of them, and their victim, the man I had risked my life to bring into this place, were caught up in a time lock that had snapped shut in 1944. I wondered if they would include me in the events, having me execute Orsini so that I would never dare to mention what happened here this day.

I pretended to have trouble hauling Orsini out. As I worked, I pulled my clasp knife and flipped it open. *"Faisez rien maintenant. Attendez!"* I whispered to Orsini. Do nothing now, wait! I slit the tape on the top side, where it was pressed against his back and would not be apparent to a casual glance.

He did not reply, but his head moved in a microscopic nod, his chin firm. I coughed to cover the click of my knife's closing and shoved it into my sleeve as I drew Orsini out of the car, keeping one hand on his wrists so they would not tear free and waste the advantage I'd given him.

"Where do you want him?" I asked.

"Here," Armand said. He gestured to a planked-in area in the floor. I recognized it as the pit from which a mechanic could work on the engine or underside of a car. I moved Orsini out onto the boards, and then Wainwright proved my theory. He stooped and removed some of the boards over the pit. There was a chain hanging from the ceiling, the block and tackle used for hoisting out engines. Armand stepped forward and looped it around Orsini's neck.

It was time to get involved. "Okay, what's going on?"

"Justice." Armand said. "A traitor to France is about to die."

CHAPTER

14

I LAUGHED as if I didn't believe him. "What are you smoking? You can't go around hanging guys."

Wainwright answered. He had the Colt in his hand now, his right hand, which he was resting on his left forearm, ready to swing his gun up and at me before I could go for my own weapon. It wouldn't have worked, not for the money. I could have put three shots into him and covered Armand before he could have raised the weapon. But this wasn't the time. The stakes weren't high enough to kill for. Not yet.

There was a normal-sized door in the wall beside the big door of the garage. It opened now, and Labrosse came in. He looked at Orsini and nodded grimly. "Good. This friend of yours did well, Mr. Locke."

"Cut the games. Armand here is talking executions. I can't stand still for that, and neither can you. You're a cop."

He drew his own pistol. Again, I could have beaten him to the draw, but only in a terminal situation. "Your gun, please."

I looked him straight in the eye. "No way." I was on the brink, and I knew it. He was a cop. He could probably concoct a story to clear himself if he shot me. I'd already established that I was a dangerous man. I'd left two hoods dead that morning. But I had a feeling about him—and about Wainwright. They could be righteous about killing as long as they stayed in their 1944 time lock, but I didn't think either one of them would kill me, not now, not in cold blood, I hoped.

For long seconds the silence in the garage seemed to echo like the aftermath of gunfire. Then Labrosse grinned and lowered his pistol. "Tough guy," he said, burlesquing an American accent. "All right, M'sieur Tough Guy. I will not take your weapon now. There will be time later, after you are an accomplice to what happens here."

"If you're going to accuse this bastard of a war crime, then you're talking a court-martial. And a soldier always has an officer working for him as prisoner's friend. I'll do the job, but I want to know what he's charged with, in English."

Armand spoke first. "He betrayed his comrades to the Germans. Men died because of him."

"And this is the first time in forty-five years that you've been able to make a case against him? Or the first time you've had someone with enough gumption to bring him in."

Wainwright spoke next. "We could live with the memory of what happened as long as it was only a memory. Captain Labrosse could live with the memory of his dead father. M'sieur Armand could live with his memories of running and fighting and hiding. I could even live with my memories of Buchenwald. But when he came back into our lives, killing Pierre and then Constance, we knew it was time to put an end to him."

"So have the captain arrest him for those two murders

and send him to the guillotine." It was worth a try. All I wanted was to get out of that garage with clean hands. I had no great affection for Orsini or for traitors anywhere, but I couldn't see him murdered.

"There is no case," Labrosse said. "So we shall try him for a case in which we know the truth, and we shall find him guilty and hang him, the way the Germans hanged so many Frenchmen."

It was getting close to the time to act. "And you're planning to do all this trying and condemning and hanging with him blindfolded. What kind of cowards are you?"

Armand took a step forward, raising his arm to strike me. "Coward? How dare you?"

"Well, if you're so brave, take his blindfold off so he can see who's calling him names." I kept a sneer in my voice, trying to make them see the childishness of what they were planning, the unfeeling cruelty of children tearing the wings off a fly.

"Very well. Remove the tapes," Labrosse said.

"Glad to." I stepped forward and hooked a finger under the tape on Orsini's face. I'd put it on carefully, making sure it didn't run into his hair. Now I patted his shoulder with my left hand and eased the tape up with my right. He stood very still while I did it, then blinked rapidly a few times and looked around at the three men. He made no sign of recognition of either Armand or Labrosse; both of them were familiar to him. But when his eyes focused on Wainwright, his head flicked in an automatic double take.

"*Oui,*" Wainwright said softly. "*C'est moi. Poirier.*" Yes, it's me. Pear Tree—his code name from the war, I guessed.

Orsini spoke rapidly in his harsh voice. I couldn't follow

it, but I had less trouble with Wainwright's response. He said he had been captured and tortured and taken to Buchenwald, where he had been liberated by British troops a few weeks before the end of the war. I also understood his closing comment, that he and Orsini were the sole survivors of the attack, the only men who knew the truth.

An important part of my SAS training had been interrogation, mostly passive, how to resist so you could hold out longer, give your mates more time to do what they'd been sent for. But I'd also been interested in the body language of the man being questioned. We'd been trained to stay cool as long as humanly possible. Orsini had not. I could read his honest surprise at Wainwright's words. He wasn't blusteringly angry; he was astonished.

He may have wanted to talk, but he didn't get a chance. Armand took over from Wainwright, cutting in angrily, delivering a long, snarling monologue that ended with a question.

In the silence after Armand's words, Orsini shrugged, then shook his head without speaking. Armand took a couple of steps forward to where he could reach the other end of the chain that ran around Orsini's neck. It looked like the trial was over and it was execution time. Time to act.

I covered my eyes with my hand as if I were overcome with the tension and half-reeled toward the car. I had left the rear door open, and I made as if to sit down on the edge of the seat that was exposed. I didn't think Labrosse would buy my collapse, but I wanted to keep Wainwright bamboozled before he remembered my ace in the hole, the booby-trapped crate of booze.

Armand paused, his hands on the chain. "The soldier cannot look at justice?" he asked, a sneer in his voice.

"This isn't justice, it's a lynching," I said, and sat on the edge of the seat, head bowed.

Wainwright suddenly got the picture. I heard him say, "Watch him!" as I turned with the case of liquor and flung it like a medicine ball straight from my chest into the garage pit, aiming the joint of the top against the lip of the hole.

It seemed to be happening in slow motion. As I threw the box, Orsini tore his hands apart and whipped the chain from around his neck. Armand was pulling down on his end of the chain so hard that when Orsini escaped he almost fell over. Labrosse and Wainwright were staring at the box, and then all of them flew backward as the case exploded in a flash of flame and a roar as loud as a fragmentation grenade.

Fortunately for all of us, it happened as the crate was tumbling into the pit, so that most of the force and the glass shards from the shattered bottles flew upward. I was the safest. I'd covered my ears and hung my mouth open as I flung the case, and I was hunched in the car so that only my side was exposed to danger. Orsini was flung the farthest, back off his planks onto the edge of the pit on my side, staggering back against the car. Armand did not get up but clutched his hand to his chest. Wainwright had dropped his gun and was too shocked to go for it again. Only Labrosse was functioning, but I had my gun out and on him before he could face me.

The scene was like a medieval nightmare of hell. The butane and cognac from my booby trap was burning like a torch, throwing a pillar of flame out of the pit. Wainwright was ignoring me, kneeling beside Armand, loosening his tie, laying him flat, feeling for a pulse in the throat. He was like some elderly saint working on a stricken sinner.

211

Only Labrosse was still acting normally, turning toward me, gun in hand.

"Drop it, Captain, and this all ends here," I shouted. He couldn't hear me. None of them could. I had saved my own hearing by covering my ears. The rest of them had taken the full shock of the blast on their open eardrums. They would be deaf, possibly for hours, but Labrosse didn't need the words, just the motion.

We stood facing one another, my gun aimed at his heart, his still pointing away in the direction his arm had been flung by the blast. Our eyes were locked, and I was cold inside at the thought that I would have to cross the line into permanent trouble by shooting him before he shot me.

Then his face changed. He almost smiled, and I caught the ghost of a backward flick in his head, over his shoulder to the great outdoors.

I grabbed Orsini by the arm and backed to the small door, covering Labrosse as I moved, although I knew it was no longer necessary. He wanted me out of there. Why and for how long, I didn't know. I shoved Orsini out and scrambled after him, pulling the door closed behind me. I was startled to see the Armands' Mercedes standing not thirty feet from the garage, with Hélène at the open driver's door. I let go of Orsini and covered the distance in two leaps, grabbing the door before she could sit back down and back away.

She raked at my hand with her nails. "You swine. You saved him."

I grabbed her hand, twisting it enough to make her buckle in the seat and forget about trying to scratch. "We're getting out. You're driving."

Orsini was right behind me, and I opened the back door and shoved him in, then scrambled in after him and stuck the muzzle of my pistol into Hélène's neck. "Let's go."

"What was that explosion? I heard a bang."

"Careless smoking," I said. "Everybody's okay. Your father's having a chat with the other guys. Just drive."

"Where?" She almost screamed it, but she was already driving, pulling her door shut.

"Just out, and don't speed. Drive at the limit. My buddy here will tell you where to go."

"That pig. They told me you would kill him. They told me to wait and drive you direct to the airport at Marseilles when you came out." She was almost screaming in her anger. "Why did you let him go?"

"Who told you to take me to the airport?" I was realizing that I'd been set up. But had they really been planning an escape for me? Or was Hélène meant to put a bullet in me? I didn't doubt she was capable of it.

"Eric." She was regaining control now, her voice at a normal pitch, weighing her words.

"Eric told you I would kill Orsini in that garage?"

Now she was in charge of herself again, talking with such confidence that there was no way of knowing whether or not she was lying. "Of course he did. This was his idea. He told us you had killed men before, that you would kill Orsini." She craned up, tossing her hair back as she angled her head to glare at Orsini in her mirror.

It didn't surprise me to find that Wainwright had set me up. I hadn't really trusted him since he let that other man get the drop on me at the farm that morning. But I was surprised about being driven to the airport. "You have an airline ticket somewhere for me?"

"To Paris. Eric says you have contacts throughout Europe, you could vanish from there."

"I'm not vanishing," I said, and glanced at Orsini. He

was trying to clear his deafness, working his fingertips in his ears, swallowing. *"Où allons-nous?"* I asked him, mouthing it large so he would be able to lip-read.

He looked at me, frowning, trying to comprehend, but before I had to repeat it, he spoke to Hélène. I wasn't sure what he said except for the word *cave*. That meant wine cellar, I knew that much.

"Pourquoi?" Hélène almost shouted the question, hammering the steering wheel with both hands. The car swerved, and she grabbed the wheel but shouted the question again. *"Pourquoi?"* Why?

He didn't answer, but he came to life now, moving forward in his seat to reach over and pick up Hélène's purse. She said something that sounded like a curse and snatched at it, but he had it high, hefting its weight. It was a nifty little Louis Vuitton number, the kind a lady would use to tote her gold card and a slim wad of thousand-franc notes. From his heft I could tell there was more than that in there.

Hélène made another grab for it, but he pulled it over the seat back and sat looking into it. He didn't search it, just removed the neat little .22 pistol from it and turned to aim it at me.

I was too quick for him, grabbing the gun and shoving him backward in the seat. He lay there, eyes blazing, as I took the magazine out. There was another round up the spout, and I cranked it out to be sure the gun was empty before reloading and slipping the pistol into my own pocket. A little extra firepower might pay off in the circle I was moving in this day.

Orsini looked at me, narrowing his eyes but saying nothing, then went back to working at clearing his deafness, distorting his face as he tried to get some reception going in his numbed ears. I just sat back and checked the road signs to try to make out where we were going.

We must have gone thirty kilometers before Hélène turned off, up a side road and then into the gateway of an unpretentious house surrounded by fields of grapes and with a steep cliff rising behind it, looming over the place so that you wondered how anybody could bear to live there for fear of rockfalls. I saw that there was a big double doorway cut into the face of the cliff beside the house.

Hélène spoke to me over her shoulder, angrily. "You know who's here, don't you?"

"No idea. I've never seen the place before."

"Amy," she said. "I left her here an hour ago. She's talking to the *patron*, some old man from the Resistance."

I glanced at Orsini, wondering what kind of a scheme he was cooking up. Did he plan to play on Amy's affection for him? To have her act as a voluntary hostage until he could get to the safety of his own rabbit warren in Marseilles and drop out of sight? His face gave nothing away. He had stopped contorting it, probably realizing that nothing but time would cure his problem.

Hélène drove up to the front door and honked the horn, loud and long, twice.

I saw Orsini's eyes crinkle in faint surprise and realized that he had heard something at last. The fact pleased him, and he sat back and waited as easily as if this were his own car and Hélène his regular chauffeur. After a little while the door of the house opened, and an old woman came out. She saw Hélène and waved and went back in.

We sat there until Amy appeared, carrying her tape recorder, frowning. She came to the car and spoke to Hélène in rapid French. Hélène cut her off and answered in English.

"Your friend Orsini wanted to see you. He came to the house with John."

Now Amy leaned down to talk to me through the window. "What happened? Are you and Eric all right?"

That was a change. I'd got equal billing with her old sparring partner. "Couldn't be better. Only I found that he and Labrosse and Hélène's dad wanted to execute Orsini for what he did in wartime, so I hauled him out of there. He asked to come here. Why don't you ask him what's on his twisted little mind?"

She shifted her gaze to Orsini, putting a smile on her face, payment, I quessed, for the introduction he had made to her latest interviewee. She spoke in French, and when he cupped his hand around his ear, she repeated herself, speaking louder and slower.

He said something to her in a voice louder than his usual growl, another sign of his deafness, and then got out of the car.

I got out on my own side and reached in past Hélène to take the keys from the ignition. She looked at me coolly but said nothing, just getting out of the car and shutting the door with a neat clunk. I noticed again how beautiful she was, even today, dressed in trim blue jeans and a white silk shirt with a couple of gold chains and dangly gold earrings as her only jewelry. She was like a fairy-tale princess, only now she was treating me like any other peasant.

The man Amy was interviewing came to the door of his house. When he saw Orsini, his face brightened like a true believer in the presence of the pope. He ducked his head and smiled and waved Orsini into the house, then, as an afterthought, the rest of us. It was a measure of his awe that he didn't give Hélène a second glance.

Orsini shook his hand graciously and went in. We followed and found ourselves in a cool room furnished with heavy old wooden items that would have fetched the price of the house itself if they'd been offered for sale in Toronto. Our host waved us to seats, but Orsini shook his head and pointed deeper into the house. The old man looked surprised but opened the far door for us, and I found out why Orsini had said *cave*. The back room led directly into the living rock. There was a natural cave here, filled with racks of bottled wine, eight feet high and thirty feet long. The cave went back a couple of hundred feet, reaching over our heads twelve to fifteen feet in places. It was sparsely lit by a few electric bulbs hanging from the bare rock ceiling. It was a natural cave that the thrifty old man had turned into his business, renting out space, no doubt, to neighboring vintners who had more wine than they had space to store it.

It was cool here, and Hélène rubbed her shoulders with both hands, hunching against the chill. I broke the silence. "What's he after? One of you tell me, please?"

"I don't know," Amy said anxiously. "I don't know what's going on at all. What was all this about the others wanting to kill him?"

"They were set to hang him, but I got him out." I was speaking quietly, but Hélène heard and made a little gesture of disgust, turning her back to me with a quick shudder that might have been contempt or a reaction to the chilly air of the cave.

"Eric wanted to hang him?" Amy repeated in a mystified voice. "He wouldn't do a thing like that."

"Did you know he was a prisoner in Buchenwald?"

"The concentration camp?" Amy gasped. "He never said anything about it to me."

I didn't wait for an answer. Orsini was picking up his

pace, walking quickly down an aisle between racks of wine. At the end of the aisle he turned sharply, lost to my sight for a moment. I broke away from the others and ran the few steps after him. He had vanished, and I jumped forward to the far side of the wine rack, crouching almost to my knees in the automatic trained movement of a soldier entering hostile space.

It saved my life again. His shot sailed over my head, through the place my heart would have been occupying if I hadn't reacted.

I dived back, behind the end of the rack, and pulled my gun. I was partially deafened from the first shot. I could make out the alarmed shrieks of the women, nothing more. If Orsini was moving, he was too quiet for me to hear. But, I realized, his hearing was in worse shape than mine. He couldn't hear me, either.

I ran back to the others, shoving the women. "Get out. He's got a gun. Get outside the house and scatter."

The old man didn't understand. He frowned at me and tried to speak to the women, but I ignored him, pushing them by the arms. "Get outside. He's dangerous." I fumbled in my pocket for Hélène's gun and gave it to her, snapping off the safety as I handed it over. "Take this."

She took it, but they kept arguing, first in French, then English, but I ignored it, keeping the pressure on until they had gotten the message and were backing out on their own, not moving as fast as I would have liked but heading for the door and safety.

By this time I had come back the full length of one rack; there were two more lengths between them and the door. I spun around the corner of the rack. Orsini was not there, and I clambered onto the top of the second rack. The top was covered with thin planking, but by stepping on the upright supports I could move without bringing down the structure, so I moved over to the far side and glanced along the length of the racks.

Orsini had vanished. That meant he was probably between the racks, waiting where the women would have to pass him. I ran, on tiptoe, along the top of the rack. The women and the old man were almost at the door, with just one more rack to pass. And then I heard them scream.

There was a sudden clatter of angry French and then a shot. I crouched, putting my hand on the top of the rack on the far side from the noise and vaulting down, knowing that Orsini would be deaf to me now after a second shot at close quarters. I ran to the end of the final rack and around it, coming out behind him as he stood with his arm around Hélène's throat, his gun trained on Amy. The old man was lying crumpled in front of him. Behind him, at chest height, a line of broken wine bottles were pulsing out their contents onto the ground, bleeding in sympathy with their owner.

I curled my fist so the barrel of my gun would not reach Hélène, and I smashed Orsini in the temple with all my strength. He collapsed. Amy screamed. Then Hélène turned and shot him, pumping three rapid rounds into his body before I could bat the gun aside.

She had fired like an expert. Orsini had three bullet holes within a six-inch circle on his chest. One of them was through the corner of his breast pocket, dead center on his heart. "That's enough," I said softly. "Pierre is avenged."

"Good," she said in a tight, angry hiss. And then she started to weep, clinging to me like a baby to its mother.

I stood, holding her, patting her back, making soothing noises, although she couldn't hear me very well, I was sure of that. I was facing away from Orsini's body, facing Amy, who was on her knees, examining the old man. She turned to me and shouted, "Never mind her. Jean is still alive. Help him."

CHAPTER

15

THERE WASN'T time to waste in waiting for an ambulance. We all packed into the Mercedes. Jean's wife crouched with him in the back, where he lay on the seat. Amy knelt next to her, keeping pressure on the wound, which was high, almost in the shoulder, and through and through. It seemed to me that the bullet had missed the lung, but I was hazy about the placement of anything else important that high up. On top of that, Jean was an old man, almost eighty. A mechanism that rickety can't take the same kind of punishment a young body can. I doubted he could make it.

Hélène used her car phone as she drove, and the Avignon police sent out an escort to whisk us into the hospital. They also alerted the surgical staff there for an emergency. The cops found us about five kilometers out of town and escorted us in, through that tangle of traffic, in a matter of three minutes instead of the forty it would have taken normally. The doctors were waiting and went to work right away.

So did the local police. Nothing brings out excitement in cops like a shooting. With Jean under the knife, the real excitement started for all of us. Jean's wife couldn't take part. She found the hospital chapel and went in there with her rosary, but Amy, Hélène, and I were the target of some very energetic detectives. They quickly gave up on me, awaiting the arrival of a fluent English speaker, but the women were both questioned at length.

After half an hour or so Hélène was given a break while the guys concentrated on Amy. I got Hélène a cup of the lousy coffee they had at the nurse's station and sat down next to her. The media people had arrived, and they were waiting down the hall with their cameras and tape recorders, but a uniformed policeman was keeping them away, so I had a chance to sit and talk to her privately. "Everything's going to be okay," I told her. "It was self-defense. No charges will be laid."

"They should be," she said tightly. "I killed him. There was no need. Perhaps he would have died from your hit."

"And perhaps not. He was a bad man. He's been bad since he was a kid. Nobody knows the evil things he's done over the years. Including killing your brother."

She looked at me now out of eyes filled with tears. "John, you try so hard to be kind. You realize that I did not want this man killed because he killed my brother."

"One reason's as good as another. He had it coming."

"I wanted him killed for business." She made the last word sound like some disgusting disease. "He was trying to ruin my father."

"He killed your brother. He's dead. That's the only thing to think about." Lord, I was getting to wonder if there was a future for me in the counseling business. Here I was in the midst of chaos, making like Dear Abby.

She squeezed my hand and then set down her coffee cup and hugged me. Not bad work, this counseling, I decided.

Someone coughed, and I looked up. Captain Labrosse

was standing a couple of paces away. "I must talk to you, M'sieur Locke."

"Of course, Captain."

I followed him down the hall past the reporters. He waved them off, and we walked to the worker's canteen, where he took a corner table overlooking the parking lot.

"You nearly killed M'sieur Armand," he said. "If he had died, I would have arrested you for murder."

"Rubbish." The English use that word a lot. It's polite, but it says it all. "I saved your neck, Captain. You wouldn't have gotten away with hanging Orsini. It would have been found out, and your career would have been over. You might have gone to jail."

"It was never intended that he hang." Now he sounded tired, Santa Claus unmasked, explaining to his son that the pretense had all been in his best interests.

"Then why did you go through all that? Why send me off after the man? You could have picked him up yourself."

A couple of cleaners approached our table with their coffee cups, but Labrosse looked up at them bleakly, and they backed off, muttering. "If I had arrested him, he would still be alive. In jail, perhaps, but soon free."

"So you wanted him dead?"

"Yes." He let the word hang there as he sat back in his chair, weary. "Yes. He was a bad man. He caused the death of many men."

It was another indication that Orsini's war career was somehow more important than the things he had done since, bad though they might have been. I took it up. "Look. Just once I'd like to get to the bottom of what's happening. Where does the division come between what's happened since Amy Roger and I got here and what happened forty-five years ago, when the war was on?" I put both hands on the table and looked at him calmly until he answered.

"It is complicated, no?"

"It is complicated, yes. I've heard Orsini accused of being a traitor to his country, of causing the deaths of a load of Resistance men, of landing our friend Wainwright in Buchenwald. And I'm personally accusing him of murdering Pierre Armand and the old lady at La Fongeline. Are the two sets of crimes tied together?"

"They are," he said, then paused while he dug into his pockets for his inevitable cigarette and lighter. He offered me a smoke, and I shook my head. He lit up, sucking the smoke down deep inside and letting it out in a long, appreciative sigh. I didn't say anything; he'd read the same medical horror stories as I had.

"That is why I let you go this morning."

"You had no choice. I could have shot you."

"You would not shoot a policeman," he said simply. "No. You are an officer and a gentleman, not a mercenary. You do not fool me, Mr. Locke."

"And you recognized all these sterling qualities and decided I should go? Or did you think that I'd end up fighting with Orsini like the rest of the world, only this time I'd kill him?"

"He was not a generous man." He brushed a nonexistent shred of tobacco from his tunic and tilted his head slightly. "I knew he would do something foolish, something that would anger you, give you no choice in the matter."

"Did you know he had arms planted at Jean's vineyard?"

Labrosse shrugged. "If not there, somewhere. From time to time we uncover arms from the war, especially in this region, where so many of our Resistance fighters were killed before they had a chance to use their guns."

"Okay, then. So you figured he would get hold of a gun and try something murderous and I would cancel his check. What did you plan to do about it, slam me in prison?"

"Hélène had a ticket to Paris for you. M'sieur Wainwright said you would slip out of sight once you got that far."

"And Interpol would ignore the warrant you issued for my arrest?"

He scowled and reached for the ashtray, stubbing his half-smoked cigarette angrily. "I would have let you go. I still will let you go. But first I have to know some things. Let me talk."

It was the first indication that he had a real agenda of his own, and I just nodded and let him go. As long as he talked, I didn't have to plan tactics, wondering whether to be on the attack or on the defensive.

"There are many things happening here," he said after a pause. "As you say, some of them reach back into the past, into the war. For the first thing, Pierre Armand was not the son of M'sieur Armand."

"But he called him his son."

"Pride," Labrosse said. "Also, he is a gentleman, something an English officer should have recognized."

If that was meant as a dig, it worked. I used to be a real pain until I served with the British army. Upper-crust Brits have a lot of faults, but their formal manners are excellent, and some of it had rubbed off on me.

"M'sieur Armand was a soldier. He spent most of the war locked up in a German prison camp. He escaped in 1944 and worked with the Resistance in Paris. When he returned home after the war, his wife was the shape of an aubergine."

"That happened a lot." It had happened to one of my

men while we were in the Falklands. I had appeared as a character witness at his trial for breaking his rival's arms.

Labrosse went on. "The story was that during the war she had sheltered a Resistance man. He had forced himself upon her, and she was pregnant."

"Orsini?" I remembered the story the old woman had told us in the little flat overlooking the square in Vaison-la-Romaine. Orsini had survived the fatal attack on the hospital. It was he who had fathered Pierre.

"But that doesn't add up." I picked out the obvious flaw in the logic. "How come he would have had his own son murdered?"

"That is what we will find out," Labrosse said. "Come."

He stood up, turning the heads of a tableful of female orderlies. French women are cool about the impact of men, they expect to draw all the admiration they need, but as much on-the-hoof maleness as Labrosse generated was going to get attention anywhere.

If he noticed them, he gave no indication. He led us back down the corridor to where the local police were talking to Amy and Hélène. He spoke to them rapidly in French and then nodded to me again and strode off to the elevator.

He took the police car, dismissing his driver to find his own way back. "We have a call to make," he told me, and there was enough force in his voice that I didn't ask questions. I just sat in and let him drive, in silence.

Once we were out of the tangle of traffic around Avignon, he put his foot down, and within half an hour we were turning into the gateway of Armand's château. He had slowed as we approached the driveway. A hitchhiker saw us and brightened as we slowed, then relaxed in disgust as we drove past him through the gates. And at last Labrosse spoke. "I want you to do something for me."

"Sure. What?"

"I want you to tell the story of what happened in the *cave*, only to make one change." We had reached the front of the house, and he stopped the car and put the hand brake on before continuing. "Instead of saying that Hélène shot Orsini, say that Miss Roger did."

"Okay, whatever you say." I wondered what he was doing but guessed that Armand's heart was in bad shape and that he wouldn't be able to take the news that his daughter was running the risk of being locked up for manslaughter.

No one was downstairs, and we let ourselves in and went up to the second floor and along the corridor to Armand's bedroom. Labrosse tapped on the door, and Wainwright opened it. He looked surprised to see us but invited us in, speaking in a low voice. "He's awake, the doctor's been."

"Good. We have good news for him." Labrosse took off his kepi as he entered the room. His hair was thin and cut very short. He clicked his heels as he reached Armand's bedside.

"I have good news," he said. "Mr. Locke will tell you."

Feeling a touch foolish but having the training to carry it through, I came to attention beside the bed and spoke clearly, as if this were a military court. "After I left your garage with Orsini, we found your daughter in the driveway with her car. Orsini asked to be driven to the *cave* of a M'sieur Jean Dupuis. There we met Miss Roger. Orsini asked Jean if he could go into the *cave*. There he took a gun from a store he had hidden. He shot Jean and threatened Hélène. I hit him on the head, and as he lay on the floor, Miss Roger shot him three times in the chest. He is dead."

Armand's face was gray, and he did not move on his pillow as I spoke, but at the end he gave a grim little smile. "Good. Thank you for telling me this."

I nodded, then glanced at Labrosse, a reaction, I guess, to see how pleased he had been with my lie. Only he was not looking at me; he was looking at Wainwright.

I followed his glance and saw that the old man was in shock. His mouth had opened in horror. He spoke to me, coaching me, appealing for me to change my story. "You mean she fired as you were attacking Orsini, don't you? That she saved Hélène's life?"

"Mr. Locke has already made his statement," Labrosse said. "I am sorry, Mr. Wainwright. I realize Miss Roger is a friend, but there is no choice for me. She must be arrested."

Wainwright was struggling to control himself. "But she will be acquitted, surely? This Orsini man had killed Pierre. He had broken the neck of poor little Constance at La Fongeline."

His words hit me like a blow. My hair prickled, and my ears roared momentarily, as if I were about to pass out. "How did you know how Constance died?" I asked. "I never told anybody."

He recovered immediately. "Of course you did. How else do you think I would have known?"

"I think you knew because you killed her," Labrosse said.

Armand's voice was weak, and he spoke in French, asking for clemency for Wainwright, I guessed, because Labrosse said in English, "No, M'sieur Armand. I cannot overlook this. It is beyond my powers. What I can do is to perhaps influence my superiors to drop the charges against Miss Roger if I get the truth from Mr. Wainwright."

He was polite but firm. "We do not wish to cause you distress. We will go somewhere else and talk. Mr. Locke will come with me, as my witness."

He bowed formally and turned to take Wainwright by the arm. "If you will come with me. You also, John, if you please."

Wainwright did not try to break away. He was acting his age now, a frail old man in his seventies, tall still but no longer straight-backed. He was weak and ill looking.

Labrosse led us down to the living room below and poured a stiff brandy. He handed it to Wainwright, who took it, nodding gratefully, and sat in a deep armchair, his body seeming to collapse to follow its contours.

"Now. The truth, please," Labrosse said.

"And if I cooperate, what then?" Wainwright asked. The cognac had given him a little color, bright dabs of red on his cheekbones, contrasting with the paleness that made his tan look sallow, liverish.

Labrosse was careful in his phrasing. "Tell the truth and I will see that no charges are laid against the young woman. She will go free. It is also possible that I can arrange for what you tell me to be charged against Orsini. He was bad. He is dead. A murder more or less does not matter."

"He is bad," Wainwright said. His voice had gained a little strength now. "Was bad, I should say. I knew that from the first time I met him."

"And when was that?" Labrosse was not taking notes, and I felt certain he was going to release Wainwright, after all.

"March 15, 1944," Wainwright said softly. "I was parachuted into the area to organize the local branch of the Resistance for an attack on the hospital."

"You were the British officer?" I couldn't help breaking in. Labrosse flicked an angry glance my way. He said nothing, but I knew I had better not speak again until his interrogation was over.

"Yes. I was dropped here to kill an RAF man who had been shot down and injured. He was a radar boffin, and the Germans had him in hospital." Wainwright sipped his cognac and paused, putting himself back forty-five years, back into his twenties, when heroism had seemed possible, even necessary.

"They caught me," he said flatly. "We found out after the war that the Germans had penetrated our organization. They picked up one after another of the people we parachuted in. Me they picked up as I landed. The Resistance hadn't got the message at all. It was the German double agent who had it. I fell into the arms of a platoon of the Wehrmacht."

"And where did they take you?" Labrosse was speaking softly. I had the impression he had waited all his life to hear this story.

"To the Gendarmerie. That's where I met your father, the man who helped me escape."

"For which he was shot," Labrosse said in the same dead tone of voice.

Wainwright had not heard him; he was reliving his own experiences. "I was tortured, of course." His hand moved instinctively to his groin, the classic starting point for humiliation and torture.

"And it was more than any man could bear and you talked." Labrosse sounded soothing.

"I still wake up terrified, sweating, even now." Wainwright gulped the last of the cognac and sat back, exhausted, dangling the glass limply. Labrosse got up and took it off him, putting it back on the table.

"And the raid proceeded as planned, only the Germans were waiting."

"It was terrible." Wainwright cleared his throat. "The Gestapo let me out for the raid. They told me to bring out all the men I could gather. It was their chance to wipe out the whole local Maquis at one swoop."

"And you did this?" Labrosse kept his voice conversational, but his eyes were burning. "You led your own men into a trap?"

"They told me they would eliminate an entire village if I did not." Wainwright had tears in his eyes. "They did it before. They did it in Lidice in Czechoslovakia, and at Oradour-sur-Glane in France, shooting all the men, burning the women and children alive in the church."

"I understand," Labrosse said. "An impossible choice. But they spared you?"

"They wanted me alive so they could bring in more people from Britain, carry out the same exercise over and over." Wainwright's voice gained strength as he spoke. I had the feeling he had lived this story in his head every day of his life, seeking to see how he could have done anything different.

"And one other man escaped. A new recruit who was so poorly trained that he didn't get into position in time and missed the trap," Labrosse said. "Our friend Orsini."

"Exactly." Wainwright had stiffened now; he was erect again. "I didn't know what had happened. I'd been told to wear a green scarf around my head, and I did so."

I looked at him pityingly. An officer, sworn to do his duty, to fight, to escape and fight again, and yet he had willingly led his men into a trap and saved his own life by surrendering again to the Germans. A brave man would have fought to the death. I felt sorry for him and the years of self-torment he had suffered since.

Wainwright went on in a soft voice. "The Germans took me alive. But they shot everyone else except Orsini. He was able to escape and hide."

"And when you were in the cells, my father let you escape also. And told you where you would be safe."

"Exactly." Wainwright pressed both hands over his mouth for long moments. At last he took them down and said, "He was a brave man, a generous man, Captain."

Labrosse ignored the comment. "The Boche shot him. Where did you go?"

"I came here, to this house."

"And who did you find here?"

"Madame Armand was alive then. She was here. So were a lot of Germans. They had taken over the château as an officers' mess. But they were behaving well; they had not harassed her. They let her live in the rooms above the stables. She hid me in the stables under the straw."

"But you did not spend all your time under the straw, did you?" I had the impression that Labrosse already knew all the answers, that he wanted only to hear them spoken out loud to silence his own midnight conversations with himself.

"No. I went out at night and killed Germans." Wainwright was proud now. "I used a knife. I killed seventeen of them in all. That was three more than the number of Frenchmen killed on the raid."

"And when you were not killing Germans, you did not stay in the straw then, either, did you?" Labrosse made his tone almost jocular. We might have been junior officers in some sociable officers' mess, kidding one of our members about his fondness for the ladies.

But Wainwright had been raised in a gentlemanly school. "I don't know what you mean," he said.

"I think you do," Labrosse snapped. "You and Madame Armand became lovers, did you not?"

"That's not something I want to discuss," Wainwright said stiffly. "It has no bearing on why we're having this discussion."

"Oh, but it does," Labrosse said. "I think that Pierre Armand was your son. *N'est-ce pas?*"

Wainwright didn't answer for a while. He glanced at me, then away, then said, "Yes. He was."

"But M'sieur Armand never knew this?"

"Marie told him she had been raped," Wainwright said, and his eyes filled with tears. "I have been ashamed of that for forty-five years, Captain. Bitterly ashamed."

"It was the kind thing to do," Labrosse said briskly. "It was better for the man to think she had no chance than to think she had conducted a love affair. You were kind, M'sieur Wainwright."

Wainwright wiped his eyes and said nothing.

Labrosse sat up. "And now we come to the events that interest me most. The events of the last few days." He paused and then wagged his finger at Wainwright warningly. "What you have told me so far means nothing. I want to know what has been happening betwen you and Orsini." He paused and then went on again in the same tone. "And do not lie as Miss Roger lied to you. I know the truth. There was no fight in the restaurant. Miss Roger and Orsini did not fight. They spent the night together."

Wainwright collapsed again, as if he'd been punched in the stomach. He did not answer for a while, and then he spoke softly. "That meeting was the start of all of this. Amy must have told Orsini about me. He already knew my name because of my connections with the wine industry here. When she told him I had been here during the war, he remembered who I was, and the blackmail began."

"What did he want?" Labrosse was brisk now, conducting the interrogation as if it had no bearing on his own personal past.

"He wanted half of everything I make. Otherwise he was going to let Armand know that Pierre was my son. That would have ruined me. Not just with him but with all my suppliers. I would have been a figure of scorn."

Labrosse rolled his eyes. "You believe that Frenchmen would have been something other than amused at *une affaire de coeur* of forty years ago?"

"It wasn't just that I had cuckolded Armand. Even he might have forgiven that, but not the fact that I had not acknowledged the boy. It was as if I were ashamed of him. That dishonored the memory of his wife."

Labrosse didn't let him slide away from the point. "So Orsini threatened you. And you had the idea that perhaps you could get someone to kill Orsini and end your problems. So you hired Mr. Locke, telling him the old story about the fight in the restaurant."

"Yes." Wainwright got to his feet miserably, picked up his glass, and took it over to the cognac bottle, but instead of refilling it, he set it down and walked on to look out the window down the long, hot driveway.

"And did you also arrange for those men to try to abduct Miss Roger the day they arrived?"

Wainwright's voice was a whisper. "I thought it would make John angry enough to do what I wanted done."

"And you were wrong," Labrosse said. "Instead, it made

Orsini angry enough to send someone to talk to Pierre to find out what was happening, to find who Mr. Locke was working for. Am I right?"

"You must be," Wainwright said, turning now to look at Labrosse angrily. "I don't know what happened after that. I don't know why Pierre was killed."

"But you do know why Constance was killed. You killed her. Tell us about that." Labrosse almost shouted it.

"It was an accident," Wainwright said, wearily sitting in the armchair once more. "I went to see her, to try and find out what was happening. I had arrived in France only the day before. She told me, and when I questioned her, she turned on me, accusing me of using Amy to get at Orsini."

"And how did this cause her accidental death?" Labrosse leaned on "accidental," and Wainwright jerked his shoulder impatiently.

"I became angry. I realized that it was her interfering, her backing up of Amy's alibi for what happened last year, that had blinded me to what had happened. I shook her as one shakes a child."

"One does not shake children that way," Labrosse exploded. "Not at all if I can prevent it, but never so hard that their neck is broken."

Wainwright raised his voice to shout down Labrosse's anger. "All right. I killed her. And then I killed her dog so the police would think some stranger had been to the house. Dammit. I've confessed! Now keep your end of the bargain. Release Amy."

I wondered what Labrosse would do. There was no likelihood that he would let Wainwright go. Too much had happened. Wainwright had caused the death of his own father and now had killed Constance. But I expected him to be honest, to level with Wainwright about Amy. He didn't. "We made no bargain," he said coldly. "My investigation continues."

"And what about me?" Wainwright asked bitterly. "You arrest me now, do you?"

"Wait here," Labrosse said coldly, and to me, "Come, we have things to do."

I got out of my chair and followed him, glancing back at Wainwright, who had risen to his feet. But Labrosse did not look back. He walked down the hallway to the stairs and back up toward Armand's room. I wanted to shout, "You're crazy. He's going to bolt," but I didn't. He knew that; I was sure of it. So I followed without a word.

By the time we reached the second-floor landing, I heard a car in the driveway, the exhaust note receding down the scale as someone accelerated away, too fast for the length of the drive.

Labrosse paused at the note, looking around, his eyes not focused on anything in the house. "He's gone," I said. "He's gotten away."

Labrosse's expression did not change. "He is a gentleman. He will do what is right," he said. Then he nodded and went on toward the bedroom.

I stood there, weighing his words. He expected Wainwright to punish himself, to take a gun to his own head. That would be the gentlemanly thing to do in Labrosse's unforgiving terms. An eye for an eye, even if you have to do the dirty work yourself. I ran downstairs and into the sitting room. The French window was open, and Wainwright was gone. Labrosse's plan, whatever it was, had worked.

The phone rang, and nobody answered for three rings, so I picked it up. *"Bonjour, c'est la maison de M'sieur Armand."* I figured my accent would deter any French person from attempting to sell me aluminum storm windows or insurance policies for my children.

It was Amy's voice. "Is that you, John?"

"Yes. What's happening there?"

"The doctor says Jean's going to make it. He's a tough old man. What's going on there?"

"Nothing much at the moment. Labrosse and Eric had a talk. Now Eric's gone somewhere in the car. I guess he's coming over to see you."

Her voice became hesitant. "Does he know about last summer? About what really happened?"

"I don't think so," I lied. Why get her into a fresh uproar? "What are your plans now? I'm finished here. You don't need a bodyguard anymore."

Another long pause, and then she said, "I guess not, but I'd like to see you."

"Okay, where?"

"My stuff's all at La Fongeline. I'll ask Hélène to drop me off there. Would that be all right by you?"

"Sure. The car's out back. I'll drive over, and we can take it from there."

There was writing paper and a pen in one of the bureau drawers, so I knocked out a note to Labrosse, telling him where I'd gone. Then I went up to the third floor and collected my bag and went around to the garage. I wasn't sure what to expect, but the first thing that came into sight when I raised the door was a fire extinguisher lying on its side. I stepped over it, looking at the rental car. It was blackened on the side nearest the pit but otherwise seemed all right. I got in and backed out of the garage—and out of the Armand family's life, I hoped.

Wainwright had left tracks in the gravel of the driveway, but I saw nothing of his car as I drove out and headed for

Faucon. There, at the top of the slope leading down toward La Fongeline, I encountered a cop directing traffic, a local policeman, not a gendarme.

He waved me back, I could not pass. I tried to explain that I was staying at La Fongeline, but he told me to go around another way. Ahead of him, rising from the vineyards below the cliff, I could see a column of dense black smoke. I didn't need anybody to draw me a picture. Wainwright had driven off the road, over the cliff.

CHAPTER

16

I LEFT my car at the gas station and walked cross-country to Constance's place, passing a hundred yards from the burned-out shell of the car. A crowd of locals had gathered, and I saw a scattering of uniformed men among them. I didn't stop. I've seen enough burned-out cars in Belfast and more than my share of dead men.

There were still gendarmes around La Fongeline, coming and going with the investigation of the morning's disaster and now of the crash. They recognized me, and I broke out a bottle of Constance's cognac and gave one of them a drink. From him I got the information I needed to lock all the pieces into place. Someone had driven over the cliff. He had been going too fast. It was suicide to do such a thing on such a road. To crown it, I learned that it had been a police car, Labrosse's car, the one Wainwright had been driving. The cops were concerned that the captain had been killed, but one of them told me that the captain was too good a driver. It must have been some new driver. The body was too charred to be identifiable.

Amy arrived an hour later with Hélène. I sat them down and gave them the news, and they both wept. Hélène invited us back to her house, but Amy refused, and eventually

Hélène went home to see how her father was progressing. She shook hands with me in a businesslike manner as she left. I guessed that Orsini's death had canceled all bets so far as our romance was concerned. It didn't sadden me unduly. Women like Hélène take too much living up to.

Eventually, the police left, and Amy and I sat in the twilight, not speaking. We had not eaten all day, but I wasn't hungry, and neither, it seemed, was Amy. She went out on Constance's patio, and I poured us glasses of wine and took them out to where she sat with her hands clasped around her knees. "Did I cause all of this?" she asked in a whisper.

"No." I didn't act hearty, the way you would with a child. She was far too bright for games like that. "This is something that's festered here for almost fifty years. Eric told me about it this afternoon. He was picked up by the Germans and tortured. Orsini was in the same outfit, but he got away. Eric ended up in Buchenwald. He had buried the memories of it all, but it was going to spring out sometime. And then Orsini killed Pierre, and the whole house of cards fell down."

"But so much happened," she said. "Twice you were attacked by people trying to kill you. Why was that?"

"Orsini," I said, happy to be telling the truth at last. "He was angry about the arrest of his men. He thought I'd been sent here to kill him. Armand's chauffeur must have told him that we were having an affair. That's why they raided your bedroom. And when that didn't work, he sent men to grab you or Hélène so I would come out in the open, where he could get at me. He wanted me out of the way. That's the kind of guy he was."

She sobbed suddenly, and I came over to crouch beside her and put my arm around her shoulders. "He was charming to you; he was exciting. You were attracted. That happens. But he was bad. He would have been bad to you at some point. You would have annoyed him, and he would have stuck you in one of his brothels without a second thought." All good, truthful stuff. It made her shudder, and then she set down her glass and said, "Hold me tight, please."

I am nothing if not obliging.

Next morning I went home. There was nothing else to do. Amy didn't need me any longer. She was going to take a room in Vaison and continue with her research. Also, she planned to be around if and when the French police released Wainwright's body. She was firm about that one, and she made one other point that endeared her to me more than anything else that had happened so far.

"I want you to know something," she said as I got into my car.

Her face was serious, so I didn't joke. "Sounds heavy."

Now she allowed her face to relax a little. "Light, I suppose, rather than heavy. I guess you know that Eric and I were very close."

"I guessed as much, but you don't owe me any explanations."

"I think I do. I hope we're going to meet again, often, when I get back home."

"I hope so, too." I squeezed her hand but stayed in the car; she seemed to need a little distance.

"Well, we were." She had a touch of her old truculence back now, and I decided it suited her. Her life was her own, not for me to pass judgment on. "Judge not, that ye be not judged," I remembered from Bartlett.

"The thing is, if he had been my real uncle, it would have been wrong," she said.

I guess I looked as if I was going to say something, because she held her hand up. "No, don't say anything. I know about the table of affinities, even if I'm not a church-goer."

"Look, this is your business."

She looked at me levelly. "It might be yours, in some measure," she said.

It was as close as I have ever gotten to being proposed to, and I pulled on her hand until she brought her face down to be kissed.

She drew back afterward and said, "I'm adopted, John. I am not a blood relation to the man I called my uncle."

I felt as if someone had lifted a ton of lead off my back. I didn't know what to say, so I winged it, meaning every word. "Listen to me. I don't care what's happened in the past. I'm going now because you asked me to. When you come home, we can get together and see what happens."

She gave me a tight little smile. "I want that. Right now I need some space—a lot's been happening."

"See you next month. Good luck with the research." I winked at her and backed out, spurting the gravel, then drove off to Lyons to start the trek home.

I stayed over in London that night and made a call to a friend of mine, a captain in the Guards, currently serving in the War Office. I figured his information might make a useful little gift for Amy when she got back to Canada.

We went through the usual chat, and then I asked him to dig into his files and find out if there was anything in the records of the Second World War about a Maquis man known as Le Loup.

He made some jokes about my turning into a scholar in my old age, and we hung up. Next morning I flew out of Heathrow and was back in Toronto around dinnertime.

There was nobody home in either of the two apartments below me. The architects on the ground floor were designing wonderfulness at their office downtown, I guessed, and Janet Frobisher had herself a date, maybe. Good for her. I hoped he was a good guy. I was feeling generous. She deserved it.

Jet lag had worn me down enough that I sat around in my apartment most of the evening, taking a little time out to head down to the basement to catch up on laundry.

As I got back to my place with the basket of clean clothes, the phone rang. It was Captain Ffolkes from London. "Been here all night, old chap," he said. I guessed he was calling from his office. "Struck oil. Your friend Monsieur Le Loup caused a lot of distress to the Hun. Killed sixteen men, all with a knife."

"Sixteen? I had a feeling it was seventeen."

"There was another victim, a Feldwebel Schmitt, but he survived. He was the only person to give a good description of his assailant." Ffolkes paused and cleared his throat, "Well, a good description may be overstating the case a little. It was dark, but he did say that the chap was short and had dark hair."

"Did he?" My eyebrows had risen an inch. That wasn't a picture of Wainwright; it was a picture of Orsini. The man had earned his place in the Maquis, after all.

"That's very interesting. I'm sure my friend here will be thrilled to get the information. Can I put her in touch with you when she gets back?"

"Oh, don't wait until then, old chap. Have her come and see me at the Warworks. I'll buy her a splendid dinner. Unless, of course, she's a particularly good friend of yours."

"Lord, you haven't changed." I laughed. "Where's your own better half these days?"

"Gone," he said. "Gone, alas, like my youth, too soon. Found a rich Yank who could buy her yachts and things that don't come easily on a captain's pittance. I still see her, of course, when he's off buying up companies, or whatever he does. In fact, we get on a lot better now than we used to when we were in harness. And she does pay the bills for our trysts. First-class arrangement. I recommend it."

We chatted for another minute or so, and I hung up. My door was still open, and I heard people on the lower stairs. It was Janet, coming back in, and she had a man with her.

Good for her, I thought. It was time somebody realized what a catch she was. I hoped he was a keeper.

I went over to shut my door and then stopped as if I'd run into an electrified fence. I recognized the man's voice.

I went out and down the short flight of stairs to her door. She was about to close it but stopped when she saw me. She was wearing what I recognized as her best dress, a green silk number.

Apparently she didn't think her date would be jealous. She bounced out the door and gave me a kiss on the cheek. She looked happier than I'd ever seen her looking.

"John, you're back. How lovely. How was France?"

I gave her shoulder a squeeze. "Interesting. Met some remarkable people."

She stood back, surprised. "What's the matter?"

"Is that our old friend Eric Wainwright in your place?"

"Yes." She was anxious now. "He's going away, John. He asked me to go with him. As his wife."

"He's going away," I said grimly. "But not someplace he can take a wife."

"What are you saying?" She was trying to come between

me and the door, but I moved her aside and pushed past into the room.

Wainwright was standing in the middle of the room. Neither of us spoke for a moment; then Janet came in and demanded, "Look, just what the hell's going on? Would one of you explain it to me?"

"Who was in that car?" I asked him. "Was it some hitchhiker?"

"It was only a German," he said. "An arrogant little Boche."

Janet stood at the door, her face drained. "What do you mean?"

"He killed a man," I explained. "I thought he was dead. A suicide, in Provence. He drove over a cliff into a vineyard, two hundred feet straight down. Only it wasn't him. It was some poor, harmless German kid he picked up on the road."

Wainwright tottered, and Janet jumped to take his arm and help him to a seat. "What's all this about?" she whispered.

"Where was he going to take you? South America somewhere?"

"How did you know?" She stood up to face me, tears in her eyes. "Eric's a good man, John. He wants me to marry him."

"He's killed an old woman in France, and now some stranger, a hitchhiker." I reached out to hold her, but she shook my hands off angrily.

"This is nonsense. Why don't you leave?"

"Don't go with him," I said. "However much you care for him, he's bad news."

"Get out." She almost screamed it. "Get out. I don't know what you're talking about. Get out. Get out!"

I went to the door, then paused to speak to Wainwright. "You're gutless. You led your own men into an ambush to save your skin. You abandoned Amy in France, even though you thought she was wanted for murder. Now you're trying to take Janet with you. You're a quavering selfish old bastard and a murderer."

Janet went for me then, flailing at me with her fists. I made no attempt to prevent it. If she thought she could be happy with this old man, it was her business. She was right to be angry at me.

I stepped back, and she shoved the door closed on me. I stood there, listening to her sobbing on the other side of it. Then I went upstairs and phoned my friend Inspector Cahill of the Mounties.

The police came for Wainwright within two minutes. I heard the voices down on the landing, and Janet's anger. She was over her tears now. Finally, I heard one of the cops say, "Okay, you stay here with him. I'll go and have a word with this Locke guy upstairs, see what's going on."

Then the other one shouted, and there was a confused clatter of voices for a minute or so and then a wail from Janet.

The ambulance arrived soon after, and I joined the neighbors downstairs as the paramedics left Janet's apartment with a stretcher.

"What happened?" somebody asked, but the guys just went on moving the stretcher, working on Wainwright as they moved. When they had gone, I went back in and climbed up to my place.

Janet's door was open, and I glanced in. She was standing in front of the shelves where she keeps her tapes displayed like books. She turned and saw me but said nothing. I watched as she selected a tape and put it into her machine.

It began to play, and she sat down, staring at the tape machine.

"Mozart's Requiem Mass," I said.

"He's had a heart attack," she said coldly. "If he dies, you killed him."

"He's already dead inside," I said. "But it happened forty-five years ago. He's been sleepwalking ever since."

"Go home," she said, and then added, "Please, John. We'll talk tomorrow."

"I'm sorry." I went over and stooped to kiss her forehead. She suddenly turned her face up to me and kissed me gently on the lips. "Thank you, I guess," she said.

"You're welcome, I guess," I answered and left, trying to work out how many days remained before Amy Roger would return from France.